"I wish you had told me I was making a mistake by marrying Josh. I would have listened to you."

"But would you have *heard* me?" Eric's mouth slid into that endearing, lopsided grin. "Come on, Molly—I've known you a long time. I know you have to make up your own mind."

But could she? She already knew she wasn't getting married, but that was all she'd figured out about her life—about her future.

Molly forced a challenging smile. "Are *you* calling me stubborn?"

His grin widened. "I didn't say you were the only one."

"I'm not. You did something none of us could talk you out of doing." *Enlisting in the Marines.*

She fisted her hands as they began to tremble. Their other friends had always teased her that he was in love with her, but they'd been wrong. If he had loved her, he wouldn't have left her when she'd needed him most.

Dear Reader,

Writing *Finally a Bride* was bittersweet for me. While I've been anxious to tell Molly McClintock's story ever since she ran out on her wedding in *Unexpected Bride* (February '08), her book is the conclusion to my THE WEDDING PARTY series for Harlequin American Romance. Molly, with her love of books and romantic nature, is a kindred spirit. Not just with me but with her best friend, Eric South. I hope you enjoy the story of the runaway bride and the man who has always been her hero.

Writing these books has been quite the challenge, as the four stories occur simultaneously. But it's been a true labor of love. As I've finished each book, I've thought it my favorite, including *Finally a Bride*. Not only does Molly get her happy ending—but so do several other residents of Cloverville, the small town in Michigan where I've spent so much time it feels real to me.

I hope you've enjoyed the time you've spent in Cloverville, too!

Happy reading!

Lisa Childs

Finally a Bride
LISA CHILDS

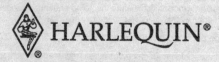

TORONTO • NEW YORK • LONDON
AMSTERDAM • PARIS • SYDNEY • HAMBURG
STOCKHOLM • ATHENS • TOKYO • MILAN • MADRID
PRAGUE • WARSAW • BUDAPEST • AUCKLAND

ISBN-13: 978-0-373-75234-8
ISBN-10:   0-373-75234-2

FINALLY A BRIDE

www.eHarlequin.com

Printed in U.S.A.

ABOUT THE AUTHOR

Bestselling, award-winning author Lisa Childs writes paranormal and contemporary romance for Harlequin/Silhouette Books. She lives on thirty acres in west Michigan with her husband, two daughters, a talkative Siamese and a long-haired Chihuahua who thinks she's a rottweiler. Lisa loves hearing from readers, who can contact her through her Web site, www.lisachilds.com, or by snail mail at P.O. Box 139, Marne, MI 49435.

Books by Lisa Childs

HARLEQUIN AMERICAN ROMANCE
1198—UNEXPECTED BRIDE
1210—THE BEST MAN'S BRIDE
1222—FOREVER HIS BRIDE

HARLEQUIN INTRIGUE
664—RETURN OF THE LAWMAN
720—SARAH'S SECRETS
758—BRIDAL RECONNAISSANCE
834—THE SUBSTITUTE SISTER

HARLEQUIN NEXT
TAKING BACK MARY ELLEN BLACK
LEARNING TO HULA
CHRISTMAS PRESENCE
  "Secret Santa"

With great appreciation to Kathleen Scheibling
for tutoring me in how to write for
Harlequin American Romance and for trusting me to
handle the challenge of writing simultaneous stories.

Chapter One

His hand shaking, Eric South replaced the cordless phone on the charger. *She didn't do it. She didn't go through with it.* He blew out a ragged breath of relief. Before he could draw another, a chime sounded. He reached for the phone again—it had been ringing off the hook all morning. But only a dial tone filled his ear.

The front door rattled as knuckles rapped hard against the wood, Eric's visitor obviously giving up on the bell. He dropped the phone and headed from the kitchen across the small, square living area to the door. As he drew it open, his heart thumped hard once, then twice. She was so damn beautiful—even in jeans and a gray zip-up sweatshirt. Her chocolate-brown curls had been tamed into perfect ringlets, held in position by the headpiece of her long white veil.

"You didn't come to my wedding," Molly McClintock said, her voice full of accusation, her wide brown eyes glistening with unshed tears.

"From what I hear, neither did you," Eric murmured.

"Eric!" She lifted her hands as if to strangle him, but instead she wrapped them around the nape of his neck and stepped into his embrace.

He was helpless to resist her, and his arms lifted almost as if of their own accord. He wrapped them tight around her, holding her as she sobbed into his shirt. She pressed close, crushing her breasts against his chest.

If she burrowed any closer, she'd be a part of him. Hell, she already was; she had been since the second grade. That was why he hadn't been able to stand up at, or even attend, her wedding. How could he watch her marry another man when she'd promised to marry him then, when they were both seven? But he couldn't hold her to a promise made almost twenty years ago.

She pushed against Eric, nearly knocking him off his feet.

He stumbled back from the doorway. "Molly..."

"Let me inside, Eric, before someone sees me," she pleaded, pushing harder.

He stepped back and she brushed past him, then closed the door, shutting them both inside his secluded log cabin. "Molly, my house isn't exactly on the main drag. No one's going to see you."

"They haven't called you?"

"Well..."

"They're already looking for me here." Panic widened her eyes even more. "I'm going to have to find someplace else to go."

"No." He didn't want her driving around the country, not when she was this upset. "I'll hide you, Molly. No one will know you're here." He'd lie for her. Hell, he'd kill for her if she asked him to.

"My car..."

"Give me the keys. I'll pull it into the garage." His garage, a barn, was bigger than the cabin.

She withdrew the keys from her jeans pocket and dropped them into his outstretched palm. The metal, warm from her body, heated his skin.

"I didn't know where else to go." Because she hadn't considered anywhere else. Molly had thought only of *him*—her best friend.

"You can always come to me," he assured her, his gray eyes intense. But then he turned and walked away. His limp was barely perceptible.

He'd probably regained his muscle tone from working out. A charcoal T-shirt defined muscles in his broad shoulders, back and arms. Faded jeans hugged his lean hips. He'd finally, two years out of the Marines, stopped wearing his dark blond hair in a brush cut and now the silky strands covered the nape of his neck.

Molly curled her fingers into her palms so that she wouldn't reach for him and beg him not to leave her if only for a little while. The door closed behind him, shutting her inside his cozy home. Alone. In the note she'd pinned to her wedding dress before she'd gone out the window of the bride's dressing room, she'd asked everyone to leave her alone—to give her time to think.

But after driving around for hours by herself, she still hadn't reached any new conclusions. She already knew what she wanted to do and what she didn't want to do.

She didn't want to get married. Not now. Maybe not ever. So why had she accepted a proposal? Why had she agreed to marry someone she hardly knew, let alone loved? She'd made such a mess—and not just of *her* life. Tears stung her eyes, but she blinked them back, refusing to shed any more. She'd already wept all over Eric. *Some great reunion.*

Since high-school graduation eight years ago, she hadn't seen that much of him. They had both left their small hometown of Cloverville, Michigan. She'd gone off to college, and he'd enlisted in the Marines. But they'd written. They'd called. They'd remained friends, even though they were no longer as close as they'd been when they were kids.

But life had gotten complicated—and it had affected them and their friendship. Eric had come back from the Middle East a changed man. Physically and emotionally.

The door opened. As Eric stepped back inside his gaze locked on her, and some of the tension eased from his broad shoulders. He'd probably expected her to run again. "I put the car in the barn and covered it up, just in case…"

"Just in case someone peeks in the windows," she surmised and sighed. "What about these?" She gestured toward tall windows, through which late-afternoon sunlight poured, brightening the log interior of the old cabin. "Do we need to get heavy drapes—or should I wear a veil?"

"You already are," Eric pointed out.

She reached up and tugged on the lace headpiece. Hairpins pulled at her scalp, which stung. "I need to take this off. Now!"

Panic, with the same intensity she'd felt at the church when she'd been about to step into her wedding dress, pressed down on her lungs. She struggled to catch her breath as she wrestled with her veil.

"Wait," Eric said, "you're going to hurt yourself."

"Too late."

Eric caught her hands in his, easing them away from the veil. "Let me help you."

"That's why I came to you." He had always been the one she'd run to—until he'd left her.

His hands on her shoulders now, he pushed her toward the kitchen and one of the stools beside the lacquered wood counter. "Sit down. Relax," he urged, kneading her tense muscles as she settled onto the stool.

"I can't until I get this veil off!"

"I'll take it off…" He pitched his deep voice low, speaking calmly, as if she was one of the accident victims he treated as an emergency medical tech and he was afraid she might be in shock. Well, maybe she was. She had been in an accident, after all. She hadn't messed up her life this badly on purpose.

Her whole life she'd always tried to do what people expected of her; she had always tried to make everyone happy. Until today.

She closed her eyes as Eric's fingers moved gently through her hair, removing the pins and loosening the veil. Her scalp tingled, not from the pins but from his touch. She struggled again for breath, but she wasn't hyperventilating now. When the weight of the headpiece lifted from her head and neck, she moaned in relief and opened her eyes to meet Eric's intense gaze.

"Thank you. You're a lifesaver." And he was. Literally. He hadn't really saved *her* life, but he'd saved so many others—in the Middle East as a Marine medic and around Cloverville and Grand Rapids as an EMT.

"I should be the one wearing the veil," Eric said, the right half of his mouth lifting in a self-deprecating grin as he pressed his fingers to the scar on the left side of his face.

"Is that why you backed out of standing up at my wedding?" Molly asked. She reached toward him and pushed his hand aside to run her fingertips along the raised ridge of his jagged scar.

Eric sucked in a breath, inhaling the scent of lilies from the flowers nestled in Molly's hair. He shouldn't have been able to feel her touch—not on his scar, but his skin warmed beneath her fingertips. He released his breath in an unsteady sigh.

"Eric, was that it?" Molly asked, her voice full of concern.

He hated pity. He didn't want it from anyone, and most especially not from her. He forced a cocky grin and said, "No, I'm used to the way my devastating good looks make people stare."

Her generous lips curved into a smile and her dark eyes twinkled as she played along. "Arrogant jerk."

"Hey, it's a burden to be this good-looking," he joked.

"You are, you know," she said, her fingertips running over his scar again. "This doesn't change that at all. In fact it probably adds an air of danger that makes women find you irresistible."

Some women. Sure. But not her. She had never found him irresistible. She'd only ever considered him a friend. He'd been kidding himself to think they could ever be anything more.

"You know me. I have to beat them off with a stick." He laughed at his own joke, but Molly's beautiful face tensed.

"Are you seeing someone?" she asked.

Just a few short hours ago she had been about to marry someone else. She couldn't really care if he had a girlfriend. So he continued to be flip. "I don't kiss and tell."

"Seriously, Eric, I don't want to stay if someone's going to be upset about my living with you."

Sure, he'd stashed her car in the barn and assured her

she could always come to him, but he hadn't actually thought she was *moving* in.

"Uh, Molly, just how long are you planning on staying?" he asked. He wasn't sure how long he could keep his sanity with her living here.

The honey-toned skin on her face turned red, and she stammered, "I didn't think—I should have asked—I shouldn't have just assumed I could stay. You have a life of your own. *You've* always known what you want."

Her. He'd always wanted her.

"I'm sorry, Eric," she continued, her words rushing together. "I don't want to mess up your life like I've messed up my own."

"Molly, you're not messing up my life."

"But I don't want to get you in trouble with your girl-friend."

"You don't have to worry about my girlfriend."

"She's understanding, then?" Molly asked anxiously. "She knows we're just friends?"

He shook his head. "You don't need to worry about my girlfriend because I don't have one."

Her slim shoulders slumped, as if she was relieved. Was it just because she felt she had no place else to stay?

"But you have a fiancé," he reminded her.

She reached for the veil that Eric had dropped on the counter and knotted her fingers in the lace. A square diamond glinted on her left hand. "I don't anymore."

"Does *he* know that?" Eric wondered.

"He's a smart guy," she said. "I think he probably figured out our engagement was over when I went out the window."

The thought of perfect little Molly slipping out a church

window had a chuckle rumbling in his throat. "*You* really went out the window? You—Molly McClintock?"

"You don't need to sound so shocked," she protested, sounding offended.

"Going out a window is something Abby Hamilton might do." He referred to another member of their group of friends, the one who had always gotten into trouble. And had occasionally gotten the rest of them into trouble, as well. He glanced down at the tattoo encircling his arm. Getting 'tats' had been Abby's idea, yet she was the only one of the friends who hadn't actually gotten "inked."

"She's back, you know," Molly said, her eyes glimmering with happiness.

"That's great. I can't wait to see her." Abby Hamilton had left town eight years ago, and she hadn't returned once to Cloverville. But since then Eric had visited her and her daughter a couple of times in Detroit and Chicago.

"You would have seen her and Lara if you had come to the rehearsal dinner last night."

But then he would have had to see Molly's fiancé, too. Not that he hadn't seen Dr. Josh Towers before. The plastic surgeon was on staff at the hospital in Grand Rapids where Eric often brought patients, via ambulance or aeromed helicopter. Eric had skipped the rehearsal because he hadn't wanted to see Towers with Molly, holding hands, kissing. Whatever people in love did.

He had never really been "in love." He didn't count the crush he'd had on Molly in the second grade and for most of the following years. But even with his limited experience, he doubted that people in love climbed out windows and left their beloved alone at the altar, humiliated in front of the entire town.

"It's not like you to take off this way," Eric pointed out. "And Abby's not been back long enough to be a bad influence on you again."

Despite the tattoo, Eric had considered Abby more good influence than bad; she had taught them all how to have fun. But Clayton, Molly's older brother, had always considered her to be nothing but trouble.

"Who was really the bad influence on whom?" Molly asked as she flashed a smile. "Abby doesn't have a tattoo."

Eric closed his eyes as he remembered where Molly had gotten hers—not that a shoulder blade was a particularly sexy spot, but she'd had to strip down to her bra so that the artist could tattoo an open book onto her skin. Because she'd been in pain, she'd wanted Eric to hold her hand.

And that was why she'd come to him now—because she was in pain. He wouldn't push her for answers she didn't have. He would just hold her hand. He reached for her fingers and linked them with his. "It doesn't matter what you did or why, you're always welcome here."

She stared up at him. "You really don't mind that I stay?"

"You can stay however long you want," he assured her.

Molly rose from the stool and pressed her body against his, sliding her arm around his back to hold him tight—as if she needed someone to hold on to to keep herself from falling over or falling apart.

His body tensed as she clung to him. One of her curls tickled his chin as her soft hair brushed his ear and his neck. He resisted the urge to pull her closer yet and press his lips to hers.

"Thank you, Eric. I knew I could count on you." She slammed the heel of her hand against his shoulder. "Even though you bailed on me. You never said why you backed out of standing up for me."

He couldn't tell her; he couldn't add to her burden. She already had one man in love with her whom she apparently didn't love back—or hadn't loved enough to marry. Not that Eric was really in love with her, but old crushes died hard. At least that was the way it was with his crush on her.

"Molly, I—"

"If it wasn't because of your scar, why did you change your mind about being in my wedding party?" Her dark eyes narrowed with suspicion. "You knew, didn't you? You've always known me so well. You knew I was making a mistake and you didn't want to be part of it."

"It all seemed kind of sudden," he admitted. She'd certainly taken him by surprise. He hadn't even realized she was dating anyone when she announced her engagement.

"Too sudden," she agreed as she pulled herself from his arms to pace back into the living room.

"So that's why you went out the window?" Because it was too soon and not because she didn't love her fiancé?

The phone jangled again, but this time Eric let it ring.

"You're not going to answer it?"

He shook his head. "It's one of them—Colleen or Abby or Brenna." Brenna Kelly, the maid of honor, had been perhaps the most upset of Molly's friends and family. She'd always been the mother of their group of friends.

"I asked them to leave me alone, so I could think," Molly murmured.

"You left a note." Abby had told him about the note pinned to the wedding dress, which had been addressed to her and not the groom.

"I just need some time. Thanks for letting me stay here until I sort things out."

Despite his dry throat, he swallowed hard and repeated his earlier question, "How long?"

She lifted her slender shoulders in a slight shrug. "I don't know…"

"You're going to need some things." Like a lock for her bedroom door, in order for him to maintain his sanity. He cleared his throat and offered, "Do you want me to swing by your house and get your mother to pack you a bag?"

She shook her head. "No. Then everyone will know where I am."

He gestured toward the phone just as the persistent ringing finally stopped. "You don't think they already know?"

Despite the sudden silence Molly continued to stare at the phone—as if waiting for it to ring again. "I'm sorry, Eric," she said, her voice heavy with regret. "I'm so sorry that I'm dumping all my troubles on you."

"Quit apologizing, Molly."

She smiled. "You hate contrition. And gratitude. And pity. Is there anything you don't hate, Eric?"

Her. He could never hate her, not even when she'd been about to marry another man. And he'd tried. "I'm a miserable old grump. Are you sure you want to stay here?"

She nodded. "I don't have anyplace else to go."

"Oh, Molly, that's not true. Your family loves you and will always support you." Her family had struggled for quite a while to deal with her father's death eight years ago, but they'd recovered and were stronger than ever. Because they'd been there for each other. Just as his uncle had been there for him.

He added, "And you have so many friends."

She pressed her palms over her eyes. "I can't face them. I let them all down—I let everyone down."

"Molly, that's not true."

"Don't," she said, her voice as hard as her gaze when she shifted her hands away from her face. "Don't lie to me. You've never lied to me."

Never to her. Only *about* her, to himself. "Then believe what I'm telling you. No one is angry with you." Except maybe Brenna, who had worked hard on the wedding since Molly had been too busy with medical school. "They're only worried about you. They want to be certain that you're all right."

On cue, the phone began to ring again.

Molly closed her eyes as if trying to retreat inside herself, to hide.

He sighed. "Maybe if I tell them you're here and you're okay, they'll stop calling."

"I don't know, Eric," she said, her voice quavering with uncertainty. "I don't know that I'm okay. But I don't want you to lie *for* me, either."

"What do you want from me?" he asked, his breath burning his lungs as he held it—waiting for her answer.

She lifted her gaze to him. "Probably too much…"

His heart rate quickened. "What do you mean?"

She gestured toward the cordless phone, vibrating with each ring on the countertop. "I shouldn't put you in this position, of having to hide me. They're going to keep bugging you."

"I can unplug it," he offered. But he'd do more. He'd always done whatever she asked of him—except once.

"No. They'll give up." Still the ringing persisted. "Eventually." Her lips lifted in a stiff smile.

"Since you don't want me to turn off the phone, what can I do for you?" Could he hold her hand? Kiss her?

"I have a suitcase in the trunk of my car, with enough things packed for two weeks."

Two weeks. "Your clothes for your honeymoon?" He bit his tongue to hold back a groan as he imagined a sexy assortment of lingerie and bikinis.

She chuckled. "Yes. Looks like I'm going to be spending my honeymoon with you."

That dream—of a honeymoon with Molly McClintock— had fueled his adolescent fantasies and kept him alive during his years in the Marines.

Now he realized why people always warned you to be careful what you wished for. That fantasy of spending a honeymoon with Molly was going to be a dismal reality, since she'd be crying on his shoulder over another man.

Chapter Two

A honeymoon. The thought of spending one with her fiancé had scared Molly as much as the marriage itself. She hadn't shared anything more than a few chaste kisses with Dr. Joshua Towers. Despite his good looks, he hadn't inspired any desire in her—no quickening of her pulse, no rush of heat. But the mention of a honeymoon with Eric instantly shortened her breath. She pushed her trembling hands into the pockets of her sweatshirt.

"You're shaking," Eric said.

She wasn't surprised that he noticed. Nothing ever escaped his attention. Apparently he'd known she was making a mistake before she had.

Unwilling to admit to another weakness, she pulled her cell phone from her pocket. "It's on vibrate."

"You should shut it off," he advised.

She nodded. "You're right." Of course. He was always right. But she'd already shut off the phone. Now if only she could shut off her tumultuous emotions—guilt being the predominant one. "I wish you had told *me*."

"What?" he asked, his brow furrowing with confusion.

"I wish you'd told me that I was making a mistake," she clarified.

"No one else told you?"

Her head still pounding from Abby's lecture the night before at her bachelorette/slumber party at her mom's, she admitted, "Abby might have said a thing or ten about my rushing into this marriage."

His gray eyes brightening with humor, he asked, "So did you listen?"

"I'm here, aren't I?" Without a wedding band on her finger; without having committed herself to a man she didn't love.

"So Abby talked you out of marrying this guy?"

She shook her head. "No." She'd come to her senses on her own. She only wished she had done it sooner. For example, before she'd accepted Josh's proposal.

"Then how could I have talked you out of it?" Eric asked.

"I would have listened to you."

"But would you have *heard* me?" His mouth slid into that endearing lopsided grin. "Come on, Molly. I've known you a long time. I know you have to make up your own mind."

Have to. But could she? She already knew she wasn't getting married, but that was all she'd figured out about her life—about her future. She shrugged off the tension tightening the muscles in her neck and shoulders. She had time—at least two weeks—to figure out her next move.

She forced a challenging smile. "Are *you* calling me stubborn?"

His grin widened. "I didn't say you were the only one."

"I'm not. You did something none of us could talk you out of doing." *Enlisting in the Marines.*

She fisted her hands as they began to tremble again, old

fear echoing in her heart. She had been so terrified she would lose him, just as she had lost her father. But Eric hadn't backed out—not even for her. And she'd begged him not to go. Their other friends had always teased her that Eric was in love with her, but they'd been wrong. If he had loved her, he wouldn't have left her when she needed him most. He wouldn't have put her through the terror of losing someone else important to her. Someone she loved.

She drew in a shuddering breath. "At least I came to my senses before I did something stupid."

Almost absentmindedly he stroked his knuckles across his scar. His voice hard with pride and his memories, he insisted, "It wasn't stupid."

She knew he spoke of the Marines, not her near-miss marriage. "I'm sorry, Eric."

"What did I say about apologizing?" he reminded her. "Quit it."

She smiled at his stern tone.

"I'm going to get your suitcase," he said, heading toward the kitchen door.

Molly ducked back into the shadows of the living room, as if someone driving by might see her. Her smile widened at her overreaction. Since Eric's cabin was off a winding private road, tucked into trees on the edge of a small lake, she doubted anyone would be driving by. But then his phone rang again. From the persistence of the phone calls, Molly was surprised someone wasn't already pounding down the door. She'd left the note. Why wouldn't they give her what she asked for—time alone?

Anger chasing away her guilt, she grabbed the ringing phone and shouted, "Stop calling!"

"Molly McClintock," a woman's voice, sharp with disapproval, admonished her. "Don't you use that tone with me, young lady."

Molly's face heating, she grimaced. "Mom, I'm sorry. I didn't know it was you."

"It doesn't matter who's calling. I've taught you better manners than that," Mary McClintock reprimanded her oldest daughter.

The last thing Molly had expected from her mother, after leaving a groom at the altar, was a lecture on *telephone* etiquette.

"You did. I'm sorry." She closed her eyes, hoping Eric hadn't overheard her apologizing again.

Music could be heard through the receiver, nearly drowning out her mother's soft sigh.

"Mom, where are you?"

"Your reception, honey," her mother answered so matter-of-factly.

"My reception?" Molly repeated, totally nonplussed. "But there was no wedding."

"We couldn't cancel the party," her mother explained. "Too many people worked too hard getting ready for it. And the whole town was looking forward to it. We couldn't disappoint everyone."

As Molly had. "I know, Mom. I'm sorry."

"I'm not the one to whom you owe an apology."

She had already talked to Joshua, the night before the wedding. It seemed the superstition about the groom seeing the bride before the ceremony was well founded. Since she'd warned him about her doubts, he couldn't have been surprised that she'd backed out of marrying him, and he wouldn't have been disappointed.

She suspected she hadn't been the only one regretting

their hasty engagement. But he had had too much honor to retract his proposal and leave her at the altar. However, he had assured her that if she changed her mind, he would understand. She had also left an apologetic voice mail for him before she'd shut off her cell. But would any apology make up for the humiliation to which she'd subjected him?

Along with music, laughter drifted through the receiver. "Who's there, Mom?"

"Everyone, honey, but you—you and Eric."

"Please don't tell anyone that I'm here."

Her mother's laugh echoed the noise of the other guests. "Okay. I won't say a word. But I don't have to."

Of course her bridesmaids knew where she'd run off to—to *whom* she had run. "Why can't they leave me alone?"

"Because they love you," her mother said, her voice warm with affection. For Molly or her friends? Mary McClintock loved all her daughter's friends as if they were her own children, but only one of them, Molly's younger sister Colleen, actually was. Mrs. McClintock continued, "They're worried about you. This isn't like you, Molly."

"I'm not sure what isn't like me and what is." She sighed. Ever since her dad had died and Eric had left for the Marines, she'd only allowed herself to focus on one thing—medical school—in order to ignore her loss and pain. "That's why I just need to be left alone."

"That's fine, honey, I'll make sure no one bothers you," her mother agreed, "but only because you're *not* alone. You have Eric."

But she didn't have Eric. He still hadn't returned with her suitcase. "Thanks, Mom."

"Sure, honey." Her mother hung up without another

word, without giving Molly a chance to ask any more questions. Everyone was at the reception. *Even Josh?*

Memories flashed through her mind. Not of her and her fiancé but of Joshua and the maid of honor, Brenna Kelly. The looks they'd exchanged at the rehearsal in the church and afterward at the dinner at the Kelly house had charged the air with the electricity of undeniable attraction. Josh and his twin sons had stayed with the Kellys after the rehearsal dinner, and Brenna had skipped the slumber party in order to play hostess to the groom and his boys. If Josh had gone to the reception, it might have been for the sake of Brenna. Molly hoped so. Then maybe some of her guilt over jilting not just Josh but his adorable sons might begin to ease.

His gaze drawn to Molly, Eric shouldered open the back door and dropped her suitcase on the floor. The thud of the heavy luggage against the hardwood startled her so that she whirled toward him, the cordless phone still in her hand. But the smile he'd witnessed when he'd stepped through the door quickly slid away from her beautiful face.

"You scared me," she accused him.

She wasn't the only one who was afraid. Eric had stayed in the barn as long as he could, steeling himself for two weeks with Molly as his houseguest—in a very small cabin. Fortunately, he had to work. That morning he'd left his supervisor a voice mail canceling the week off he'd previously arranged because he'd thought he'd be too distracted—by thoughts of Molly married to someone else—to work. Then, after backing out of the wedding party, he'd realized he would *need* the distraction of work.

"Did I scare you?" he asked. "Or was it whoever you just talked to?"

"No, it was you," she said. "You've often scared me, Eric."

"Then I guess that makes us even."

She narrowed her eyes as if confused. But she never had really understood him—not in the way he understood her.

"So who was on the phone?" he asked, gesturing toward the cordless as she replaced it on the charger.

"My mom."

He couldn't help but smile. He loved Mrs. Mick, as Abby Hamilton had dubbed her years and years ago. Everyone loved Mary McClintock, although not like her husband had loved her. Eric knew all her kids—whether they admitted or not—wanted the deeply loving relationship their parents had had.

"Is she mad?" he asked.

Molly shook her head, tumbling those chocolate-colored curls around her shoulders. "No. You know my mom. She understands."

"Yeah, she's pretty great."

"You're pretty great, too," she said, "for letting me stay here."

"It's no problem," he lied. He reached for the suitcase again, his muscles straining as he hefted the weighty tweed bag. "You might change your mind when you see my spare room, though." But he didn't lead her there. Instead he stopped in the doorway to his own room.

Molly's heart bumped against her ribs as she collided with Eric's back. "I thought you were putting me up in the *spare* room."

He dropped her suitcase then shrugged, his shoulders rippling beneath the thin cotton of his T-shirt. "I can't put you in Uncle Harold's old room."

"Why not? Is he coming home?"

His shoulders lifted as he drew in a deep breath. "No."

He expelled a heavy guilt-ridden sigh. "But every time I visit him at the VA hospital, I let him think that he will."

She reached out to brush her fingertips along his forearm. "He's not the only one who wants to think he's coming home."

"No, he isn't," Eric admitted. "I want him here, so I've left all his stuff where it was."

"I won't touch anything, I promise."

"No, it's not that. Hell, he hardly has anything *to* touch. Career soldiers travel light," he explained.

Thank God Eric hadn't followed completely in his uncle's footsteps. He hadn't made a career of the military. Her gaze skimmed over his scar. Had that been *his* choice, though?

"Guys in the service that long don't accumulate a lot of stuff," he continued. "But then, Uncle Harold didn't need much."

"No, he didn't," she agreed. "He had you."

"He didn't need me, either," Eric dismissed himself.

She hated when he did that. Realizing that she still held his arm, she squeezed it gently and his muscles tightened beneath her grasp. "He was lucky to have you in his life."

"I was lucky he took me in," Eric said, his voice betraying the emotions he struggled to suppress. "My parents barely knew him."

Harold South was actually Eric's father's uncle, his great-uncle. With few other relatives alive, his parents had named friends, another married couple, as their son's guardians in the event of their deaths. They had probably never considered the possibility that Eric might actually have to live with his guardians, and they couldn't have envisioned the car accident that took their lives when their son was only four. He'd lived with the guardians for a few years, but then their marriage disintegrated and neither had wanted the responsibility of a seven-year-old boy. Fortunately, since his parents' funeral, Uncle Harold had been keeping track of Eric. And he'd taken Eric in when no one else had wanted him. Molly knew that was the way Eric had interpreted the situation—that no one had wanted him.

"He loved having you live with him." She reminded her friend of the joy he'd brought to his uncle's life. "He wanted you sooner, but he didn't feel it was his place to fight your parents' wishes."

So how could she fight *her* parent's wishes? How could she disrespect her father, the man who'd meant more to her than any other man—except Eric? She winced as her head pounded, the ache probably generated from stress and too little sleep the night before her wedding day.

"You're exhausted," Eric said, as always changing the subject from himself. "Take my bed."

Heat rushed to her face. "I can't!"

Not without remembering the last time she'd been in it—when she'd thrown herself at him, begging him not to leave her for the Marines.

He turned toward her, his eyes widening at her sharp tone. "Molly…"

"I can't take your bed." Not unless he lay in it with her as he had that night, the last night before he'd left her. "That's asking too much of you." And of her. But then it wouldn't be the first time someone had asked too much of her.

Eric shook his head. "I can't put you up in there. I haven't even opened the door in over a year. It's a dusty mess."

"So I'll clean it. It's fine," she insisted as she backed away from the doorway.

Molly hadn't even stepped inside his room with him, but

Eric's heart pounded hard. Before picking up the suitcase again, he glanced once toward the bed. Memories quickened his pulse, but he pushed away the traitorous thoughts. He'd accepted long ago that he'd never get Molly McClintock back in his bed. If only she had come to him that night because she'd loved him—as a woman loves a man, and not just as a friend who hadn't wanted to lose him.

Hinges creaked as she pushed open the door on the other side of the living room. Unlike Eric's room, which Uncle Harold had added when his nephew came to live with him, the old man's quarters were original to the small cabin. Eric joined her in the doorway, where dust particles danced in the late-afternoon sunshine that came streaming through the sagging blinds.

"Come on," he said. "You can't stay in here."

"It's fine," she insisted, her eyes watering. She sneezed and then giggled. "Well, it will be once I clean it. Put down my suitcase and show me where your feather duster is."

His arm straining, Eric hefted her bag onto the bed. More dust rose from the faded flannel comforter. Where before he hadn't wanted to know, hadn't wanted to envision her in any skimpy little honeymoon lingerie, now he had to ask, "What do you have in that thing? Bricks?"

"Maybe you're just getting weak," she teased, skimming her fingertips over the barbed-wire tattoo on his bicep.

He shoved his hands into his pockets so he wouldn't reach for her, so he wouldn't drag her into his arms and tumble them both onto the dusty mattress. "Seriously, Molly, what do you have in there?"

Giggling again, she stepped around him and unzipped the steamer trunk–size suitcase. "Books."

"You packed books for your honeymoon?"

She lifted her shoulders in a shrug and kept her head bent over the bag so he couldn't see her face. "I like to read."

"You *love* to read," he corrected her. "You've always loved to read." Everyone in Cloverville was aware of that. She was known as the McClintock who had her nose forever in a book.

"That changed a bit when it came to medical school," she said as she dropped several paperbacks onto the flannel comforter.

"Textbooks kind of dull?"

She made another sound—not her usual carefree giggle but a bitter chuckle. "I prefer fiction."

His own bitter memories—of the places he'd been, the things he had seen—washed over him. "Yeah, me, too." And not just because of the past but the present, too. His dreams of a honeymoon with Molly had been much more exciting than the reality.

She pulled an assortment of long dresses, jeans and a sweater from the suitcase.

"Where the hell were you going for your honeymoon?" he asked. "The North Pole?"

She tossed a wide-brimmed straw hat atop the pile of books and clothes. "I wouldn't need the hat there."

"Where were you going?" he asked again, then shook his head. He didn't need an image of her and the *GQ* doctor lying together on some white sand beach or tangled in satin sheets. "No, it's probably better that I don't know."

A bell pealed in the kitchen as the phone resumed ringing. He groaned. "I should answer that or they'll keep calling."

"I thought they'd stop," she murmured as she followed him.

"Me, too. Brenna called my cell while I was in the barn, getting your suitcase."

"You talked to her?"

He nodded.

"How mad is she?"

He gestured toward the phone. "I guess madder than I thought."

"You lied to her?"

"Not exactly. I just didn't offer any information." He picked up the cordless and barked into the receiver, "Yeah?"

"South?" his boss asked, his voice flustered with confusion.

"Yes, Steve. So you got my message? Do you need me to come in?" *Please, God.* His body tensed when Molly brushed against him as she headed back toward the bedroom with the bucket of cleaning supplies he kept under the sink.

Steve chuckled as if Eric had said something particularly funny. "Leave it to you to want to work on your day off, South."

"It's no problem. Really," he assured his supervisor. "I don't need the time off anymore."

"Your wedding get canceled?"

"It wasn't *my* wedding." It wouldn't have been—he'd accepted long ago that he would never marry. "But, yeah, it was canceled. That's why I left you the voice mail saying I wouldn't need my vacation time. And if you want me to come in right now..."

"No, Eric, that's not why I called. In fact, I called for the exact opposite reason."

"You're firing me?"

Steve laughed outright, the phone crackling with his raucous chuckle. "I'd like to clone you, not fire you."

"Then I don't understand…"

"I've already made up the schedule for next week, and I'm leaving you off it."

"But I don't need the time off." Especially now, when he had such a distracting houseguest.

"Yes, you do, Eric. In the two years you've been working for me, you haven't taken a single day off. Not a personal day. Not a sick day and none of your vacation time."

"I like my job." He couldn't help Uncle Harold—or the comrades he'd lost in the Middle East. But as an EMT he could help other people. Sometimes.

"I'm glad you like your job," Steve said, "and I want to keep it that way. You already arranged for the week off, and I'm going to make sure you stick to it."

"But I don't want to."

"But you need to, Eric. You need to take some R & R or you're going to burn out. I've seen it happen too many times. I don't want it happening to you." He laughed. "Hell, I can't afford to have it happen to you."

"I appreciate your concern, but I'm fine."

"So take the time off and stay that way," Steve insisted. "Everyone's been warned. No calling you to work for them, either. I don't want to see you back here for a week, South. That's an order. I know that you're too good an employee to disobey an order." But the supervisor must have doubted him because he hung up before Eric could begin to argue.

Molly ducked her head out of the bedroom doorway. "I take it that wasn't one of my bridesmaids?"

"Not this time." He sighed. "Seems like I'm going to be around more than I thought next week." More than he'd hoped.

"That's good," she said, but she sounded about as convinced of that as he was.

"Don't worry, though," he assured her. "I'll stay out of your way. Give you time to…read." Maybe he would have to borrow a few of her books. Anything to get his mind off the thought of her here, lying in a bed just a few yards away from his.

"Hmm?" She turned toward him, obviously distracted.

"Nothing," he said. "Your mind is somewhere else." Or on someone else. Did she regret running out on her groom?

"They didn't cancel the reception, you know," she informed him.

"I know," he admitted. "Your bridesmaids have been calling from the American Legion." The post was the only facility in Cloverville big enough for parties. Even if the new construction expanding the town included a banquet hall, he doubted any true Clovervillians would use anyplace but the American Legion. The town, like his uncle Harold, was loyal and steeped in tradition.

She groaned. "Didn't Abby read them the note?"

"You didn't ask them to leave *me* alone," he pointed out.

She grinned, amused by their friends' ingenuity. "Leave it to them to find a loophole."

"To find you."

"Even though they know where I am, I think they'll leave me alone for a while," she said, her earlier panic seeming to have subsided.

"If they let you be, it's probably only because of your mom." Mrs. McClintock would make sure the others laid off.

"Probably," she agreed.

"I guess it doesn't matter why—as long as they agree to do it," Eric allowed.

Molly glanced up at him and blinked, as if she hadn't heard a word he said.

"That's what you want, right?" he asked, wondering if she'd changed her mind. "Time to think?"

"Yes," she said vaguely, leaving Eric to consider whether she was answering his question or another one she'd asked herself.

"If you'd rather be completely alone, I can take off," he offered. "I have a buddy I can crash with in Grand Rapids. I stay with him when I work doubles. He's closer to the hospital." Maybe that would be far enough away so that he wouldn't think of her. But he doubted it, since even the Middle East hadn't been far enough away.

"I don't want you to leave." Her dark eyes shone as if something had just occurred to her. "At least I don't want you to leave without me."

"I know I'm going to regret asking," he said, his stomach muscles tightening as he braced himself for her response, "but what exactly do you want, Molly?"

She flashed him a smile as her eyes took on a mischievous glint. "I want to crash my wedding reception."

Chapter Three

"This is crazy," Eric grumbled as he handed Molly a glass of punch. But he'd gone along with her plan—just as he always did.

Fighting a smile, Molly tilted her head so she could see beyond the brim of her hat. Eric's face was also in shadows because of the fedora he wore. In a dark pin-striped suit, with his hat and a bright red tie, Eric resembled the dapper gangsters of old. Dashing but dangerous.

"You look good," she murmured, pitching her voice low so no one would overhear.

As usual, he didn't acknowledge her compliment. "You look like Mrs. Hild."

The elderly widow whose life revolved around her roses… She wore flowered dresses and wide-brimmed hats. Molly smiled. She didn't exactly consider the comparison an insult. She had always liked the town busybody who lived on Main Street. The hand-carved Cloverville Town Limits sign was planted in the front yard of her little Cape Cod right beside her flowers.

"You were really going to wear *that* on your honeymoon?" he asked, his voice full of the same disbelief that had been on his face when he'd seen the contents of her heavy suitcase.

She bet *his* bride wouldn't bring books, or much of anything else, on their honeymoon. If she had Eric, she wouldn't need anything else. Her heart clutched at the thought of Eric marrying another woman—any woman but her. Not that she wanted to marry Eric; they were only friends. Despite that night before he'd left for the Marines, that was all they'd ever really been.

She lifted the glass of punch and sipped from the rim, then coughed. She had asked for nonalcoholic, but after he'd worked so hard to get her a drink, sneaking his way over to the bowl, she couldn't reject what he had brought her.

"What's wrong with this?" Molly glanced down at the long loose-fitting flowered dress she wore. "I like it."

And that was all she'd considered when she'd packed for her honeymoon, what she liked—not what her new groom might appreciate. She hadn't thought about him at all. Guilt tugged at her. Poor Josh. What a horrible woman he'd picked for his bride. She hoped he'd choose a better one next time. She hoped that next time he'd propose out of love, and not from the desire to find a mother for his twin sons.

And she hoped that the woman to whom he proposed would accept out of love—and not just from a desire to escape the choices she'd previously made. Of course Molly had thought she could love Josh. And despite not seeing all that much of his sons, she'd thought she could love Buzz and T.J., too. The four-year-olds made her think of what Eric must have been like at their age, when he'd lost both his parents, not just his mother.

"And the hat?" Eric asked, flicking a fingertip against the brim and snapping her attention back to him and the present.

"The sun is bad for you, you know," she maintained. But she wasn't quite sure why she'd packed the hat. She hadn't even known where they were honeymooning, just as she hadn't known much about the wedding.

She glanced around the American Legion Hall, its whitewashed paneling and worn linoleum complemented by well-placed white-and-red fairy lights and balloons. White linen tablecloths covered the dark laminate tables where the townspeople ate fish dinners every Friday in the spring. Her mother had been right. Everyone, and most especially Molly's maid of honor, Brenna Kelly, had worked hard to make the wedding and reception special—beautiful.

Everyone had worked so hard on her wedding—everyone but her. She hadn't been able to focus on it because she'd been wrestling with another tough decision.

"With your complexion, you don't burn," Eric persisted, unwilling to drop the subject of the hat. "You tan."

"The sun is still bad for you," she maintained. She hadn't needed to attend medical school to learn that. Maybe she hadn't needed to attend medical school at all….

"Did we come here to discuss the sun?" Eric asked, wondering how they had gotten onto that topic when what he really wanted to know was why she'd talked him into crashing her wedding reception. Then he added, with admiration for Molly's hard work and determination, "Dr. McClintock."

The playful smile drained from Molly's face, which paled despite her honey-colored skin. He glanced around, thinking maybe she'd seen someone who upset her. But no one stood around where they loitered in a short hall leading only to a fire exit. Everyone was on the dance floor—enjoying Molly's reception. Was that what upset her?

"I'm not a doctor," she said, her voice unusually sharp and defensive.

"Not yet," he agreed, lifting his glass of punch to his lips. "But you will be soon."

She shook her head. "I'm not so sure about that anymore. I've dropped out of med school."

He blinked, more stunned by her admission than by the sip of punch he'd just taken. Someone had spiked the non-alcoholic punch bowl. He glanced around for her kid brother, Rory, and the Hendrix boys, Rory's usual partners in crime. But then he returned his attention to her, half closing his eyes as he studied her face. He could not have heard her right. "What did you say?"

"I dropped out," she repeated. "I quit medical school."

He shook his head. "I thought you were just going to take a little time off—for the wedding."

"That's what I thought, too," she said, her eyes darkening with anxiety. "But I'm not sure I can go back."

Had her wedding just been an excuse to quit medical school? Was that why she had accepted a marriage proposal from a man she'd only dated a few short months? No wonder she'd backed out. She had obviously come to her senses.

"Molly—"

"I don't want to talk about it," she stated, lifting her chin defensively. "Not now."

Maybe not ever, Eric thought. After all these years, had she finally changed her mind about becoming a doctor? He should have been surprised, but he wasn't. He hadn't ever believed she'd decided to be a doctor because *she* wanted to. Had she done the same thing with her wedding? Agreed to marry because it was what someone else wanted, and then run away when she'd realized it wasn't what *she* wanted?

"Molly..."

"Come on, let's dance," she implored, winding her arm through his to tug him toward the dance floor.

He dragged his feet on the worn linoleum, resisting her, just as he had when she'd begged him not to join the Marines. "Someone will see us."

"They won't recognize us in these outfits. I'm so glad you found your uncle's old hat." She placed her punch cup on a tray, reaching for his glass next to add to the pile of discarded dishes.

Eric touched the brim of the well-worn fedora, then ran his fingertips down the side of his face. "It doesn't cover this, so it's not much of a disguise."

"Then I guess we'll just have to dance cheek to cheek," Molly said, her lips curving in an impish smile.

Eric's body tensed, even though he knew she was only teasing. So he teased back. "Not with that big floppy hat of yours," he said, touching the brim. "The way we're dressed, we're far more likely to draw attention to ourselves than disappear into the crowd. Do you want people to see you?"

"No, but I want to be able to see what's going on and I can't see *anything* from back in this hallway. Come on." She tugged on his arm again, pulling him into the reception hall. "I think you're more worried about being seen than I am."

She was right. She probably thought he was self-conscious because of the scar, but that wasn't the reason. Even though he didn't know how he would weather two weeks with Molly, he'd resigned himself to spending her "honeymoon" with her. Platonically, of course. But if someone saw her and convinced her to come out of hiding, she wouldn't need to stay with him.

Worse yet, she might decide to stay with *him,* her jilted groom, and have a real honeymoon—even though she'd skipped the wedding.

"I'm just worried that you haven't thought this through," Eric said.

She stopped at the edge of the dance floor and turned toward him, admitting, "I've given you good reason to worry about me, the way I ran away from my wedding and let down so many people."

"They don't look too let down," he said, pointing toward all the dancing couples. From the hospital, he recognized the *GQ* doctors. The blond best man, Nick Jameson, held a brunette tight in his arms—Molly's younger sister, Colleen. And the jilted groom, Dr. Joshua Towers, danced with the maid of honor, Brenna Kelly. Towers grinned at the redhead, neither of them looking too upset. How would Molly feel about that—that the man she'd been about to marry wasn't destroyed by the fact that she'd abandoned him at the altar?

"That's why I had to come here." Molly tilted her head, so she could peer out from beneath her hat brim. "I had to see if I was right." Relief eased some of the tension from her shoulders.

"Right about what?"

Brenna and Josh. But she didn't want to tell Eric that she hoped her fiancé had fallen for her best female friend. She didn't want him thinking…well, the truth. That she'd been about to marry a man she didn't love. Because then she would have to explain why—that she was a chicken. She didn't want Eric to be as disgusted with her as she was with herself.

Molly scanned the rest of the guests on the dance floor, gasping in surprise as she noticed a certain couple doing more than dancing. The dark-haired man leaned over the small blond woman who was in his arms, kissing her as if he never intended to stop. Molly grabbed Eric's arm. "See—"

"Abby and Clayton?" he asked, whistling through his teeth.

"And you thought I was crazy for wearing this long dress. I suspected it might be cold in here, but even I didn't realize that hell was going to freeze over."

Eric laughed. "Man, seeing that almost makes it worth dressing in this crazy getup. I'm seeing it and still not believing it—Clayton and Abby?"

Molly giggled at his shock. "Men can be so oblivious."

"Are you talking about me or Clayton?" he asked, his mouth lifting in a partial grin. "I always thought he hated her."

"He wanted to," Molly explained. "But…" She'd always suspected that attraction, not animosity, existed between Abby Hamilton and her older brother, Clayton.

"That's not hate," Eric mused. "I can't wait to razz Abby about this."

"You can't say anything to her."

"That's right—we're not supposed to be here." His hand closed over her elbow, steering her back toward the deserted hallway.

Her skin tingling beneath the thin material, she pulled away. "We can't leave yet. It's just getting good."

Eric gave her a long, assessing look. "You planned this," he accused.

She shook her head, and the floppy brim of her hat fluttered. "I didn't plan." A smile tugged at her lips. "Hoped, maybe."

That was why she'd left her note addressed to Abby, asking her to stay until Molly came back. She wanted her friend to move back to Cloverville—for good.

Eric grinned. "You're a chip off the old block."

"What?" Her heart clutched at his grin and his words, but she knew he was wrong. She wasn't like either of her parents. She wasn't strong, like her father, who had stayed so brave even when he was so sick—or like her mother, who had survived having to watch the man she loved dying, unable to help him, to save him. Even though many years had passed since her father's death, the memory of that feeling—that sense of utter helplessness—was still as oppressive as it had been the day he'd died.

That helplessness was part of the reason she had decided to become a doctor. She hadn't ever wanted to lose anyone else she loved because she was unable to save them. She gazed up at Eric, and her heart shifted again. She'd nearly lost him, too—the best friend she'd ever had.

"You're like your mom," Eric explained as she studied him with an odd expression, a mixture of confusion and something else he couldn't name. "You're a matchmaker."

But her mother's matchmaking had never succeeded. Despite all her efforts, Mary McClintock hadn't ever managed to make her daughter see Eric as anything but a friend. He pulled his attention away from Molly's beautiful face to focus on the couple on the dance floor, but they weren't a couple anymore. Clayton stood alone as Abby pushed her way through the other dancers to escape him. Molly's matchmaking wasn't any more effective than her mother's, it appeared.

"Matchmaker? Who? Me?" she asked, widening her eyes in feigned innocence.

At least she probably thought she was feigning it. To Eric she was innocent, full of optimism and hope—qualities he'd forsaken long ago when he lost first his parents, then his guardians. If not for Uncle Harold bringing him to Clover-ville, he wasn't sure where he might have wound up, bounced from foster home to foster home.

He certainly wouldn't have ended up here, crashing a wedding reception with the runaway bride. "Hmm… I guess it's true, that whole thing about returning to the scene of the crime," he murmured.

"Crime?" she asked. "I'm not admitting anything, but since when is matchmaking a crime?"

"Since you set me up with Trudy Sneible for homecoming our sophomore year." When he'd brought up her crime, he'd actually been referring more to her running out on her wedding than coming to the reception. But he didn't want to make her feel worse than she already felt; he preferred her mischief making to the heart-wrenching tears she had sobbed when she'd first showed up at his door.

"Trudy was cute," she defended their old classmate.

"She was." Not as cute as Molly had always been, though. "She was also six feet tall, and I hadn't had my growth spurt yet."

"You were a squirt," she reminisced.

"She about trampled me on the dance floor."

Molly's fingers wrapped around his hand, and she tugged him into the midst of swaying couples. "Dance with me. I promise not to trample you."

"I'm not worried," he lied. He wasn't worried about her physically trampling him; she probably didn't weigh much over a hundred pounds, while he'd finally had that growth spurt in his junior year of high school and was now six foot himself. But he *was* worried about her trampling him emotionally.

He could not fall for Molly McClintock again. He was

too old for unrequited crushes, and he had even less to attract her now than he had back in school. He couldn't compete with the handsome and successful doctor.

Not that he wanted to compete. He had learned long ago that if you allowed yourself to feel anything, you opened yourself up to pain. It was better to feel nothing at all.

"If you're not worried, why are you way over there?" Molly asked as she stepped closer, settling her breasts against his chest. She tipped her head back to look up at him, knocking off her hat in the process.

Eric caught the straw monstrosity and clutched it against the back of her head. "Someone's going to see us," he warned her just as a couple dancing near them slowed their steps.

Two elderly women, holding hands, danced to the waltz the deejay was playing, probably at their request. One wore a hat as wide as Molly's, but hers had flowers, wilted now, covering the brim.

"Damn," Eric murmured. "We're busted."

Molly drew his attention away from the town busybodies as she slid her palms up his chest to clutch his shoulders. Then she pulled herself up until her soft lips brushed his. Eric's heart slammed against his ribs and his hand, still on her hat, clutched her closer. Summoning all his control he kept himself from deepening the kiss, from taking it further than he knew she intended it to go.

Her mouth slid from his, across his cheek, across his scar, and she whispered in his ear, "Are they still watching us?"

"They never were."

Was Eric right? Had she kissed him for nothing? Her lips tingling from the all-too-brief contact with his, Molly pressed her fingers to her mouth. Had Mrs. Hild and Mrs. Carpenter not noticed her, *them,* at all? When she pulled out of Eric's arms, she hadn't seen the old women. Of course she'd been too distracted, with her face all hot with embarrassment, to focus on anyone but Eric.

She had murmured something to him before she'd run off the dance floor, away from him. For the moment. Until she went home with him. How could she go home with him now—after she'd kissed him?

Of course he probably hadn't thought anything of it. He would have realized why she'd done it. He was Eric—he knew everything about her. He knew her better than she knew herself.

She stood in front of the cake table. Someone, probably Mr. Kelly, had sliced up the infamous Kelly confection. Crumbs of chocolate and smears of buttercream frosting marked the plates left on the table. The top tier hadn't been touched except for the bride. She was gone. The plastic groom stood alone atop the last piece of cake.

Would Josh have done that in exasperation? Had he thrown away the bride? While she'd never seen him as anything but kindhearted and patient, her desertion might have driven him to react strongly. After all, she wasn't the only woman to break a promise to him. His first wife had abandoned him and his sons shortly after the twins were born. Poor Josh. She winced with a pang of guilt over humiliating such a nice man.

Accepting Josh's proposal had been a mistake. She'd wanted to be a mother to his sons, but she had no experience with children. Unlike Brenna and Molly, she hadn't babysat any kids other than her younger siblings. The time she'd spent with Buzz and T.J. had been awkward—she hadn't known what to say to them and they hadn't talked to her at all. Josh had assured her that they only needed to get used to her. But it was better that they hadn't. They wouldn't miss her.

Would Josh? He'd intended to move both his practice and his home to Cloverville. For her, or for his sons?

Fingers, knotted with arthritis, wrapped around her wrist. "Molly McClintock, I thought that was you beneath that great big hat."

Molly closed her eyes as the heat of embarrassment rushed to her face again. "Mrs. Hild…"

"And I suppose that was Eric South *dancing* with you." From the delight in the older woman's voice, she had undoubtedly witnessed more than the dancing.

For a moment, vindication lifted Molly's spirits—she'd had every reason to kiss Eric. Then she remembered that she had been caught, just as Eric had warned her she would be. He had been right. Again.

"Please, Mrs. Hild, don't tell anyone you saw us," she implored the other woman.

"Honey—"

Of course, how could she expect the town's busiest body to keep this delicious gossip to herself? "I know it's quite the story, the bride crashing her own wedding reception, but I'd hate to hurt anyone—" emotion choked her voice "—any more than I already have."

Mrs. Hild's grasp tightened on Molly's wrist. "Honey, somehow I think *you're* hurting the most."

Apparently Eric wasn't the only one who knew her better than she knew herself.

"I'm fine," she insisted, because she had her pride. Well,

as much pride as a runaway bride crashing her own wedding could have. "Really."

"Your secret is safe with me," the elderly widow assured her.

Somehow Molly suspected those were words Mrs. Hild had never spoken before. And yet Molly believed her. "Thank you."

"So who do you suppose stole the bride?" the woman asked as she, like Molly, stared at the top of the cake where the groom stood alone.

Despite breaking her promise to marry him, Molly doubted Josh had been angry enough to throw away the plastic bride. No, probably someone had snitched it as a joke. Probably the same someone who had spiked the non-alcoholic punch.

"Rory." Molly smiled with affection for her naughty teenage brother, despite his tasteless prank.

Mrs. Hild shook her head, and the flowers on her hat brim bobbled. "No. I don't think it was that boy."

Molly turned from the cake to study the other woman's gently lined face. Mrs. Hild's pale blue eyes sparkled with another secret. "You know," she realized. "So tell me. Who took her?"

The widow lifted her bony shoulders in a shrug. "I didn't *see* him do it."

"But you have your suspicions," Molly prodded.

"Oh, I *know*."

"So tell me," Molly urged, "who stole the bride?"

Mrs. Hild closed one faded eye in a wink. "Eric South."

ERIC RUBBED his hands, which were wet from the running faucet, over his face. Then he gripped the sides of the por-

celain sink and stared into the mirror above it. With that
scar, he had a face only a mother could love—and he'd lost
his mother a long time ago. Molly had kissed him just to
hide their faces from Mrs. Hild and Mrs. Carpenter. He
knew that. He'd known it the moment her lips had brushed
his, but still that hadn't stopped him from reacting, from
desire rushing through him, heating his blood and harden-
ing his body.

Hands shaking, he shoved them into the water again. As
he lifted them toward his face, the door creaked open
behind him. He glanced into the mirror—not at his own
face this time, but at the face of the man who'd just entered
the lime green–tiled bathroom.

While not so much as a shaving nick marred the perfection of Dr. Joshua Towers's face, a frown knitted his
brows. He pushed open the empty stall doors before
turning toward Eric. But Eric pulled his gaze away and
stiffened his back and shoulders, mentally erecting the no-
trespassing sign he'd been accused of using before, to
keep people from getting too close.

Towers ignored the sign. "Uh, sorry to bother you…"
His voice cracked with an odd laugh. "Sounds funny for
me to say sorry to someone else…"

"Been getting a lot of that yourself?" Eric asked, reaching
for the fedora, which he'd set on a metal shelf beneath the
mirror. Not that he needed to disguise himself for this man.
As a plastic surgeon Towers didn't spend much time in the
E.R., where Eric brought patients. And while Eric had seen
him a couple of times before, they had never officially met.

"Yes, I've been getting a lot of apologies." The jilted groom
sighed. "Which is crazy, you know, when no one did anything
to me. They have no reason to feel sorry about anything."

"Maybe they feel sorry *for* you," Eric pointed out.

"They have no reason for that, either. But you're right," the groom admitted with a heavy sigh. Then he added, "They feel sorry for me." Towers focused on Eric, on the part of his face that everyone focused on as if unable to look away.

Eric touched his scar. "I get a lot of that myself."

"I don't know how much you know about me…"

More than he cared to. "That you got left at the altar, but you must not be that mad about it since you attended the reception anyway."

Josh laughed again. "Oh, my best man thinks I'm mad—the crazy kind of mad."

From what he'd heard around the hospital about the best man, legendary bachelor Nick Jameson, Eric figured Nick had thought his friend crazy to consider marriage in the first place. He wasn't wrong.

"Why did you come?" he asked.

Had he hoped that Molly would show up, having changed her mind about marrying him? Was that why Molly had wanted to come—*had* she changed her mind?

Eric would understand if she had. Towers had a lot to offer a woman. He was successful, rich and handsome, with no obvious scars. But since Eric's real scars weren't on the outside, he didn't know that for certain about Towers.

Josh shrugged. "I told my best man we had to attend the reception—which got changed to an open house, then a welcome-home party for Abby Hamilton—because we need to get to know our potential patients. We're opening a medical practice in town. Maybe you'd like to make an appointment. We could discuss some options for dealing with your scar."

Eric, almost absentmindedly, brushed his knuckles across the ridge of flesh on his cheek. "I know my options."

"I'm a plastic surgeon," Towers explained. "It's my specialty."

Eric already knew that if anyone could repair the damage to his face it was Dr. Josh Towers. The guy was quickly becoming a legend for the relief he'd brought burn and accident victims. But Eric didn't feel like a victim.

So he changed the subject. "When you came in, you were looking for someone or something."

Molly? But why would she be hiding in the men's room? Eric was hiding in here from her.

"Yeah, I didn't want to bother you, though. You seemed pretty intense."

Josh wasn't the first person to think that. Apparently even his boss had thought so, since the man had insisted Eric take his vacation, forcing him to spend time with Molly. It didn't matter how long Eric hid in the bathroom, he would have to face her eventually. Guilt nagged at him; he wasn't having the easiest time facing the groom, either.

"Can I help you with something?" he asked.

"Did you see two boys, about this high?" Josh asked, dropping his hands to within three feet of the floor. "They look kind of like me." Dark-haired and blue-eyed, then. "One has a buzz cut and the other one has spiky hair."

Eric shook his head, but concern made him ask, "Are they lost?"

"They gave Pop and Mama—Mr. and Mrs. Kelly—the slip."

Pop and Mama. Towers already referred to the maid of honor's parents by their nicknames. Of course, Eric had heard that Towers and his boys were staying with them, but

Eric detected real affection more than simply gratitude in the other man's tone.

Knuckles rapped against the door before it pushed open a crack. A woman's husky voice drifted through the small space. "Josh, I found them."

Eric slapped the hat on his head and pulled the brim low over his eyes, just in case Brenna stepped inside. He wouldn't put it past her to enter the men's room. The maid of honor was one of the boldest women he knew.

Josh sighed with relief. "Thanks." More than gratitude filled the word as his attention turned to the door, which hid Brenna from Eric's view but obviously not Josh's.

"They're sleeping in the coatroom," she said. "Do you want to take them home?"

"Home…" Josh murmured, his voice soft with awe and acceptance.

Eric suspected he now knew why the other man had attended the reception for his canceled wedding. For Brenna.

How would Molly feel about her fiancé's attraction to her best friend—her best *female* friend? Did she suspect? Was that why she'd backed out of the wedding but still wanted to attend the reception?

"Think about that appointment," Josh advised Eric as he stepped through the bathroom door to join Brenna.

They had probably just exited the hall before Molly, still wearing her ridiculous hat, slipped inside the men's room. "Are you okay?" she asked.

Unable to lie, Eric just nodded. "You?"

Molly sighed. "I'm ready to go home."

Home. Was that how she thought of the little cabin on the lake, which Eric had struggled for so long to accept as his home?

"Did anyone see you come in here?" he asked, a smile twitching his lips as she cast surreptitious glances at the urinals.

She shook her head. "I don't think so."

"You didn't pass Brenna and Josh in the hall?"

"I watched through a crack in the ladies' room door until they left," she explained. "They didn't see me."

He sighed. "Even if no one saw you come in, they're going to notice you coming out of the men's room."

Especially in her silly disguise. He caught a glimpse of himself in the mirror. His ensemble wasn't much better.

She turned toward him, her dark eyes shimmering with humor. "Nobody's going to see me come out of here."

He hated to ask, but he had to know. "Why's that?"

"We're going out the window."

Chapter Four

"Hurry," Molly urged Eric, her pulse racing with excitement. "Lift me up."

"If I push you through that window, you're going to fall into the alley and land on your head," he pointed out. "I thought you had experience going out windows."

"Just one," she said as she tipped her head back and stared at a narrow window high on the bathroom wall. "And that was only a couple of feet above the floor."

"You're going to have to go out the way you came in," Eric insisted, gesturing toward the door.

Molly shook her head. "Someone will see me."

"And you don't think they saw you walk in here?"

She thought she'd been careful to duck inside the men's room when no one was looking—since she hadn't exactly been comfortable about doing it in the first place. But she'd gotten worried about Eric, especially when she'd seen Josh join him.

"Someone might have seen me," she admitted. Or Mrs. Hild might have broken her promise. "That's why I have to go out this way."

"Molly…"

"Stop arguing and lift me up."

Eric stared at the window, assessing her chances of getting through. "You're going to have to climb onto my shoulders."

At the thought of climbing all over Eric, Molly's heart beat faster yet. But she shook her head in protest. "All I need is a boost."

"Molly, you can't just jump out. You have to consider how you're going to fall."

Was he talking about this window or the one she'd already gone through? Did he think she hadn't looked before she leaped?

"I'm glad you backed out of the wedding party," she said with a disgusted snort. "If you'd been at the church with me, I would have wound up getting married by the time we got done arguing over *how* I'd go out the window." She jerked on his arm. "Hunker down so I can climb on you."

Eric's breath audibly caught, but he bent down and hunched his back. Molly wrestled with the skirt of her long dress, bunching it around her thighs so she could swing one leg over Eric's shoulder.

"This wasn't so hard when we were kids," she mused, a smile lifting her lips as she remembered all the piggy-back rides Eric had given her over the years.

"No, it wasn't this hard when we were kids," he agreed. His warm palms settled against Molly's bare thighs, holding her on his shoulders as he straightened up. "Are you sure you can't just go out the door?" he asked, his voice strained.

Molly knocked off his hat and clutched his soft hair with her fingers. "I'm going to fall."

"I've got you. Don't worry…"

Ironic coming from him, when he was the one about

whom she worried the most. She had almost lost him once, and the fear that she might lose him again would forever haunt her. She lifted her hands from his head and reached for the transom window, pulling it open far enough for her to squeeze through.

"Boost me up just a little more," she directed.

"And we always accused Brenna of being the bossy one," Eric murmured. His hands tightened on her thighs as he lifted her.

Her skin heated and tingled beneath his touch while her heart pounded hard. She held her breath as she squeezed through the opening, holding on to the brick ledge above the window.

"You okay?" Eric asked. "You're not stuck?"

"It's tight," she murmured as she tried to settle her butt on the sill. "I'm glad now that I didn't have a piece of cake."

"Molly, this is crazy…"

Before she could form an argument, her fingers slipped from the bricks above the window and her butt slid off the sill. She fell back, free form, with her hands outstretched, grasping only empty air.

"Molly!"

Grimacing, she tensed, preparing for impact with the asphalt. Instead, she bounced painlessly onto empty boxes and tinfoil tubs of banquet leftovers. Mashed potatoes, gravy and rubbery chicken successfully cushioned her fall.

Eric's head poked through the window, and he peered down into the Dumpster where she'd fallen. His face stark in the light from the flood lamps illuminating the alley, he asked anxiously, "Are you all right?"

Molly dragged a badly needed breath deep into her

lungs, but then she coughed and sputtered, choking on the odors from the trash surrounding her. Hers weren't the only leftovers in the Dumpster.

"Molly?" The window shuddered as he jammed his shoulders into the opening. To no avail. He couldn't fit through.

A door opened onto the alley.

"I'm fine," she whispered, waving him back into the bathroom. Moving slowly she shifted around on the garbage so that she could crouch down and peer over the metal edge.

Brenna and Josh stepped into the alley, each of them carrying a sleeping twin. Molly blinked as her heart warmed at the thought of the beautiful family her friends could have. If they took a chance on love…

A bottle shifted beneath her foot and she knocked against the side of the metal container.

"Whatttt?" one of the twins murmured as he shifted in Brenna's arms.

"Shh," she soothed the groggy child. "It was nothing."

"A rat," Josh teased.

Her tone haughty, Brenna informed him, "Cloverville doesn't have rats."

Molly could have argued that—she felt like a rat for the way she'd treated her friends. Brenna had worked so hard for the wedding, and Josh had to have been humiliated. But if love came out of this, it would be worth it.

Molly wouldn't have screwed up everyone else's life, then. Just her own…

She glanced to the bathroom window, looking for Eric. But he was gone, not even a shadow shifting behind the glass. The garbage, however, shifted again beneath Molly's weight. She sank deeper, mashed potatoes—at least she hoped it was mashed potatoes—oozing between her toes and over the tops of her sandals.

"That's a rat," Josh insisted.

"No, it's probably a raccoon," Brenna suggested, coming to the defense of her hometown.

A car door opened, and the boys grunted and murmured protests as Josh and Brenna settled them on the backseat. An engine rumbled to life. Molly held her breath against the stench. She only had to wait a couple minutes more....

"I should go inside and let Pop know about the scavenger," Brenna said.

"The raccoon?"

"Yes, I wouldn't want Mama or Mrs. George to stumble across it when they're cleaning up."

"I can take care of it," Josh offered.

"Oh, you can?" Brenna challenged him. "You have a lot of experience dealing with raccoons?"

"I've always lived in cities. I have experience dealing with rats. Isn't that all a raccoon is—a big rat with a striped tail?"

The door opened again from the reception hall. Molly braced herself for the maid of honor's surprise at Eric's presence, but instead a booming voice vibrated off the brick wall. "You're still here? The boys are sleeping— they need a soft bed."

"Pop, there's something in the Dumpster," Brenna explained. "If Mama found it…"

"She'd scream the whole town awake," Pop concluded, "and things are just starting to wind down."

"Sir—"

"Pop," Mr. Kelly corrected Josh.

"Pop, I can help you."

"Nonsense, that'll be the day I can't take care of a critter," Pop said, his big hands gripping the edge of the Dumpster. "But if I needed help, I think I noticed ole Harold's nephew…"

His eyes widened as he met Molly's imploring gaze. She lifted a finger to her lips. *Please, don't say anything….*

Not that she didn't deserve more than her share of humiliation.

"What is it, Pop?" Brenna asked.

"Nothing," the older man murmured before winking at Molly. "You two need to get out of here. Take those boys home. Look at their necks, all crooked like that…."

"Pop's right," Brenna admitted.

"Where's my recorder when I need it?" her father teased. He waved them off. "I'll see you back at the house before too long. Everyone's clearing out now. We'll be cleaned up in no time," he assured them.

Pop stood beside the Dumpster, waving, until Josh's Suburban pulled from the alley. Then he reached a hand over the rim to Molly.

"Thank you," she said, trying to hold her breath as she put her hand in his and climbed up the side. She was just about to vault over the top when the door opened again. Tugging her hand free of Pop's, she dropped back inside the metal container, crunching cardboard and tinfoil beneath her once more.

"I thought that was you," Pop said to someone as he slapped him on the back.

"Pop," Eric acknowledged the other man with warmth and the easy familiarity of long acquaintance. "Wh-what are you doing out here?"

"Me?" The older man chuckled. "I'm getting a *raccoon* out of the Dumpster."

"Ra-raccoon?" Eric stammered. "Uh, why don't you let me handle that for you."

"Thought you wanted nothing to do with this wedding, son?" the older man teased.

"Pop—"

The old man slapped his hand against Eric's shoulder this time. "Don't worry. I know why you're here."

That made one of them. Eric still had no definite idea why Molly had wanted to crash her own wedding.

Molly's head popped over the edge of the Dumpster, and she extended a hand toward him. "He knows I'm in here," she said. "He covered for me with Brenna and Josh."

Eric closed his hand around hers and pulled her onto the edge of the trash container. Then he wrapped his hands around her waist and lifted her down onto the asphalt. Even with her clothes rumpled and coated with garbage, she was gorgeous—especially since she'd lost the godawful hat, so that her chocolate-colored curls were free to frame her heart-shaped face.

"You okay?" he asked, his stomach still clenched with the horror that had overcome him as she'd dropped out of the bathroom window. He hadn't been that scared since the Middle East.

She nodded, dislodging a broccoli floret from her tangled curls. "I'm fine."

"How the heck did you wind up in there, girl?" Pop asked, shaking his head in bemusement.

Eric began to answer for her. "She was in the men's—" until a small elbow jammed into his side.

"I was hiding."

"I think you could have found a better place," the older man commented, green eyes alight with amusement.

Molly wiped a streak of gravy from her arm. "Definitely. But I think it worked. I don't think Josh and Brenna saw me."

Pop shook his head, his hair all black but for a shock of white falling across his forehead. "You're lucky Brenna didn't climb inside to take care of the 'raccoon' herself," he said, with pride in his daughter.

"Pop," Molly implored the older man, "you won't tell anyone that you saw us?"

"That's your secret to keep or share," he said. "I trust you have your reasons for everything you're doing?"

Teeth gnawing her bottom lip, she nodded.

"I've known you since you were in diapers, Molly McClintock," he said. "I know you'd never purposely do anything that would hurt another person."

"She wouldn't," Eric agreed.

Pop flashed him a grin and patted his arm. "If you had any doubts, girl, you did the right thing by not marrying your doctor."

"Some people don't belong together," she said by way of explanation.

Pop's grin widened as he considered the two of them. "And some people do."

"Do you need help cleaning up?" Molly asked Mr. Kelly, as if anxious to change the subject. "We can help you."

He shook his head. "It's under control, honey. Most of the guests have left, but there are enough still here that your secret will be out if you go back inside. Especially since Mrs. Hild is hanging on. You know that old busybody can't keep a secret to save her life or anyone else's." While he chortled at his joke, Molly gasped.

"You're sure, Pop?" Eric asked.

"You know old Rosie Hild…"

"No, about cleaning up," Eric explained. "You're sure you've got it?"

"Of course. You did enough this morning, helping me load the cake into the van." His bright eyes narrowed as he studied Eric.

Eric resisted the urge to squirm beneath the older man's scrutiny. He wasn't exactly proud of what he'd done that morning. It had been childish, and he hadn't often acted like a child since his parents had died.

"The cleanup's almost done. You need to get Molly… wherever Molly's staying." Pop turned toward her. "Are you going home, honey?"

She shook her head. "I need some time alone to think."

Eric resisted the urge to snort in derision. Despite Molly's claim to want time alone, she'd insisted on crashing her own wedding reception.

The older man patted her shoulder, far more gently than he had Eric's. "You'll figure things out, honey. You're a smart girl."

The door had barely closed behind Pop's back, before Molly erupted in laughter.

"What?"

She gestured at her dress and hair, which were filthy from her Dumpster dive. "He thinks I'm smart?"

"You are—"

"I'm crazy. I climbed out not one but two windows today. I just swam around in what's left of my wedding-reception buffet. I've totally lost it, Eric."

Her eyes bright with humor, she'd never been more beautiful to him. She wasn't the only one who'd lost *it.*

SOFT HAIR DRIFTED over Eric's face as he lay back on a lounge on the deck off the kitchen. He dragged in a deep breath that was scented with strawberries and champagne. What a dream…

"Do I still smell like garbage?"

Molly's voice jolted him back from where his mind had drifted, when he'd allowed himself to focus on the mental image of her in his shower, standing naked under the pulsating spray—her hands lathering soap all over her body as she washed every inch of silky skin….

"Eric? Are you sleeping?" she asked, dropping onto the edge of the wide chair. Her hip bumped his thigh, and every muscle in his body tensed with desire.

"I could have fallen asleep. You were in there long enough…." Torturing him with the images her showering had conjured in his mind.

"You didn't have to wait up for me," she said. "I don't expect you to entertain me while I'm here."

"What *do* you expect from me?" He asked the question that had been torturing him as much as her naked image.

She lifted her legs, bare but for the boxer shorts that barely reached midthigh, and stretched out beside him, tight against his side. "Just you, Eric. That's all I expect from you."

Friendship. That was all she had ever wanted from him. He sighed and lifted his arm, curving it around her bare shoulders. Her head settled onto his chest, her hair brushing his chin. "No."

Molly's face tilted toward his. "No?"

"You don't smell like garbage anymore." A grin teased his lips. "But if trouble had a smell…"

"I'm sorry."

He caught her chin in his free hand. "What did I tell you about that? No more apologizing."

"But I dragged you to the reception, after making you get all dressed up."

He sighed. "I'm used to it. You used to do that when we were kids—make us get all dolled up to act out some play you'd read."

"And Brenna would be the director." Her breath hitched. "Do you think she's very mad at me?"

He shook his head, but he didn't say what he really thought about Brenna—that she was falling in love with Molly's ex-fiancé. Although Towers wasn't actually Molly's ex yet. They hadn't officially broken up; Molly still wore his engagement ring.

Hell, maybe Eric had only imagined the attraction between Brenna and Towers. The doctor had probably actually attended the reception in the hope that Molly would show up there.

Eric's arm tensed. While he'd been in the service he had seen too many guys lose the loves of their lives to other, more available men. Eric had vowed then never to be either man in that equation—not the one left by the woman or the one stealing the woman.

"It's late. We should head off to bed," Eric suggested.

Molly's head shifted on his shoulder as she burrowed closer. Her lips brushed his throat as she agreed, "It is late."

"You're half-asleep."

"No. I'm wide awake. I think I'll stay out here and watch the sun come up over the lake." She draped an arm around his waist. "You don't have to stay with me. I'll be fine alone."

God, he wished he could leave her alone....

Chapter Five

Awakened by the first peal of the doorbell, Molly hovered in the shadows of the living room as Eric stumbled toward the front door. A fist hammered at it now, the visitor impatient. Molly shouldn't have expected them to give her any peace. This was Cloverville after all. And apparently Mrs. Hild couldn't keep a secret. Or had Pop given her up—or worse yet, Mom?

The only person she could really trust was Eric. He wore drawstring shorts, his heavily muscled chest and legs bare but for a patchwork of thin scars. Her heart clenched at the pain he'd clearly felt—the pain she remembered feeling herself over him.

No, Eric was the last person she could trust. He had already hurt her; she couldn't trust him not to hurt her again, even more.

"You want to hide?" he asked, without even turning toward her. How had he noticed her? Because Eric never missed a thing....

Had he missed her when he'd been in the Marines for six years?

She shook her head but shifted closer to the wall. Eric

drew open the door, planting his foot behind it as if to discourage a salesman.

The door pushed against his arch. "Good morning, Eric," Molly's mother greeted him with a pat on his unscarred cheek. "You look tired, honey," she observed with concern. "My daughter keep you up late?"

They had stayed awake all night—until the rising sun had streaked the sky with pink and orange, which had reflected on the dark water of the lake.

"Hello, Mrs. McClintock," Eric said, stepping back from the door as she pushed her way inside the small living room.

"Is my daughter still sleeping?" she asked, then turned and spotted Molly. "There you are."

"I'll just go put on some coffee," Eric murmured, backing away from the women as if wanting to avoid a messy confrontation.

Molly had brought entirely too much drama to his quiet life at the cabin. With a stressful job such as his, as an EMT, he probably needed peace in his downtime. She had disrupted that.

Her mother's head turned, following Eric's retreat to the kitchen. Then her attention refocused on Molly, her big brown eyes widening as she took in her daughter's attire. "Did I interrupt anything?" she asked.

When the air had chilled the night before, Eric had given Molly his shirt, which she wore over her cami and boxer shorts. "No, Mom, this isn't what it looks like…."

Mary McClintock sighed and shook her head. "That's too bad, honey."

"Mom!" Molly shot a glance to the kitchen, to see if Eric had overheard the comment. She only caught a glimpse of his bare back, muscles rippling as he reached for a tin in the cupboard. Maybe her mother was right. Too bad…

Her mother's fingers closed around her chin, pulling Molly's attention back. "Mmm, hmm…" Her eyes glittered with a matchmaker's delight.

"No," Molly insisted. "It's not like that…."

When he'd left for the Marines Eric had proved that he considered her nothing more than a friend—no matter what everyone else had always believed.

"Why are you here?" she asked. Then she peered out the window to where her mother had parked her minivan on the driveway. "Are you alone?"

Mom nodded. "Abby's off on a run through town. Colleen's hanging out at the park—hopefully with that handsome best man who came calling for her early this morning. And Rory and Lara are home watching cartoons."

"Best man? Nick Jameson came calling for Colleen?" Concern for her younger sister stiffened Molly's spine. "And you told him where she was?"

When Molly had volunteered at the hospital, she'd heard things about Jameson—not very flattering things about his arrogance and his predilection for purely superficial relationships. Colleen had volunteered at the hospital longer than Molly had, so surely she had to know Jameson was not to be trusted.

"Your little sister's a big girl. Bigger than you," Molly's mother pointed out with a grin. "She can take care of herself."

So her mother was obviously more worried about Molly than her sensitive sister? Then she had reason to worry, because Molly had never acted more out of character than she was right now.

"Why are you here?" Molly repeated. "I told you I need time…"

"I know. I know," her mother assured her. "But you also need food. I brought some wedding leftovers for you."

"I already had a few of those," Molly admitted. The shower had washed broccoli, gravy and mashed potatoes from her hair. She touched a riotous curl and wished for a brush. The scent of her strawberries-and-champagne shampoo drifted around her nose…along with the scent of cinnamon. "Did you stop at Kelly Confections? I thought they'd be closed today."

"Some of Brenna's staff were working at the store today. They open on Sunday mornings now."

"Do I smell cinnamon rolls?" Eric called out from the kitchen.

Water gurgled as the coffee brewed, the rich aroma mingling with the cinnamon. Molly's stomach growled. She couldn't remember when she'd last eaten. She'd pretty much lost her appetite the minute she'd accepted Josh's proposal.

"Because I know you have a sweet tooth," her mother said as she walked toward Eric in the kitchen, "I also brought you some cake."

Eric bussed a kiss against the older woman's cheek when she joined him at the counter. With curly dark hair like Molly's and eyes just as wide and warm, she was like a living age progression of her beautiful daughter. "That's why you're my best girl, Mrs. Mick. You're joining us for breakfast, right?"

Blushing, she shook her head. "No. I have to get back home. I don't quite trust Rory as a babysitter."

Did she trust *him?* Eric studied the older woman's face. He knew what she must have thought when he'd opened the door. He was only wearing shorts, Molly was in his shirt, and they were both rumpled with sleep. Since she had found an excuse to stop by, she obviously didn't trust him. He couldn't blame her. He'd been tempted last night to give Molly more than his shirt.

But she was still engaged to another man. She needed time to sort out her feelings; she didn't need *him* as anything more than a supportive friend.

Mrs. Mick touched his face again, patting his scarred cheek this time. "You keep an eye on my girl, Eric. Make sure she's really okay."

"I am okay," Molly insisted. Then, bristling with pride, she added, "No one needs to keep an eye on me."

"Sure, honey," her mother said with gentle condescension. In a flurry of movement Mrs. McClintock stowed food in Eric's copper-toned refrigerator. Then she kissed and hugged both of them before rushing back to her van.

"What was that?" Eric murmured as he splashed some coffee into a mug.

"A bird. A plane. Nope. Supermom," Molly joked, bumping her hip against Eric's as she helped herself to coffee.

His house was too small for the two of them. If they kept rubbing up against each other, he might forget that he was supposed to be only a friend.

"I'm sorry about her barging in like that," Molly said.

"Sorry about what? She filled the fridge." Eric bit off a gooey chunk of cinnamon roll. He could handle that Kelly Confection. But he wasn't sure he could touch the wedding cake. *Again.* "She's a sweetheart."

And Molly, more than any of the other McClintock children, had taken after her mother. She always tried so hard to please everyone else. Had she ever really taken time for her own pleasure? Maybe that was what she needed to figure out—what would make her happy? Eric's guts twisted as he acknowledged that, from everything he'd heard about him, Towers would have made Molly happy, if she had given him the chance.

"Yeah, she's pretty great," Molly said with a smile. "Poor Colleen, though. Sounds like Mom's trying to play matchmaker with her and the best man."

"The way they were dancing last night, your mother might not have to work too hard on that," Eric reminded her.

"I hope Mom's right, and I don't need to worry about my little sister," Molly said, gnawing at her bottom lip again.

"You're infringing on Clayton's territory," he admonished her.

"How's that?"

"He's the McClintock who worries about everyone else."

"He needs to worry about himself," Molly said. "I'm sure our matchmaking mother has been giving him hell since Abby's home."

"Especially if she saw that kiss last night." Eric couldn't help but smirk, remembering all the times Abby Hamilton had insisted she hated Clayton for being humorless and bossy. "I can't wait to give Abby hell myself." He owed it to her for all the times she'd teased him about Molly.

Molly bumped her shoulder against his arm, right where the barbed-wire tattoo encircled his bicep. "You can't. Remember we promised not to bring it up."

That wasn't the only thing they'd promised not to bring up again. Eric's muscles tensed as he remembered the night eight years ago when they'd made that promise. Because he couldn't indulge in memories, not now, not with her living with him, he pushed the past aside and pretended to gripe, "You're no fun, Molly McClintock."

"You're right." She sighed. "I stopped being fun a long time ago."

"You stopped *having* fun," he qualified. "Until last night. Didn't you enjoy dressing up in a disguise and crashing your own wedding reception?"

"Sure," she said with heavy sarcasm. "The Dumpster diving was my favorite part."

"Mine, too," he admitted, grinning. "You looked so cute with mashed potatoes in your hair."

"You weren't laughing when I went out the window," she reminded him.

Eric's scar twitched as his grin faded. "I'm probably not the only one not to laugh when you went out a window yesterday."

Molly sucked in a breath as if he'd sucker punched her. And in a way he had. But he had to remind himself about Towers, that even though she hadn't married him, she must still have some feelings for her fiancé. Or she wouldn't have accepted his proposal in the first place.

"I shouldn't have said that," he admitted as shame gripped him. She was his friend. She had come to him for support, not derision.

"Why not?" She shrugged. "It's the truth. I trust you to always tell me the truth."

He wouldn't lie to her, but over the years he had learned to keep some things to himself—such as hope. "I know Mrs. Mick wants me to keep an eye on you—"

"I don't need a babysitter," she insisted. "You don't have to watch me."

The problem was that he couldn't stop himself from watching her. He needed some space. "If you're sure."

"I'm sure."

"There's something I do every Sunday…."

"Then do it," she urged him. "Don't let me disrupt your life any more than I already have."

"Molly…" He couldn't lie. She had disrupted his life. "I'm going to take a shower now. Don't eat all the cinnamon rolls."

"Eric…"

He turned back, and his heart clenched at the forlorn expression on her beautiful face.

"If I'm in your way, I can leave," she offered.

"Are you ready to leave yet?" he asked.

Her dark brows furrowed with confusion. "What do you mean?"

"Have you figured out what you want to do?"

She shook her head.

He swallowed a sigh. "Then you better stay until you figure it out."

Years ago he had hoped that one day she'd figure out she loved him. But now it wouldn't matter if she did. He couldn't love her back. His old crush had died with all his other dreams…when he had nearly died in the Middle East.

ERIC CAST a sideways glance at Molly as they walked up the steps of the veterans' hospital. He'd wanted time to himself and distance from her.

"You really don't mind that I'm coming along?" she asked.

He'd been looking forward to that drive alone from Cloverville to Grand Rapids, to an hour of solitude to regroup and some necessary miles between him and his tempting houseguest. But he shook his head.

"I haven't seen your uncle in so long," she said.

"He probably won't remember you," he warned her. "He usually doesn't remember me."

"I understand. I know a little about Alzheimer's."

"Of course. You're the med student."

Tension etched a deep line between her brows, and she said, "Not right now."

"Are you going to go back?" He couldn't believe she would give up a dream she had spent eight years chasing, even if he had given up *his* dream of being with her.

"I don't know what I'm going to do."

"Is that something—" along with whether or not she would marry the man she'd left at the altar "—you need time alone to think about?" Not that she seemed all that eager to spend time alone.

"I have to think about my whole life." She expelled a weary sigh. "I think I'm beginning to question every decision I ever made."

He reached out, brushing his knuckles across the back of her hand. "If you need someone to talk to…"

"I have you."

She had had him. For so many years.

But then he'd gone away from her and Cloverville. And he hadn't come back—not completely. He'd left a piece of himself in hell. And he was never reminded of that more than when he came to visit Uncle Harold.

Wheelchairs lined the halls, some of them sitting empty outside darkened rooms. Most of those chairs were occupied by old soldiers who fought now—against age and ailments.

Dread tightened his stomach into knots. Was this his future? His dream for anything more than what he had had been destroyed—along with too many good soldiers. Soldiers Eric should have been able to save.

"Sergeant South," murmured an elderly man who stiffly reached out a hand to grasp Eric's arm. "It's good you came to see the major."

"Isn't he doing well?" Eric asked, bending over to search the corporal's face. Corporal Underwood's mind was sharp despite his failing body. Did he know something about Eric's uncle's condition?

"He's fine, boy, and although the old major gets confused I think he instinctively looks for you every Sunday afternoon."

Molly suspected Eric's uncle wasn't the only one who looked forward to his visits. The corporal had stationed himself in the hall, as if waiting for Eric. His watery gaze slid to her.

"You're running a little late today," he said, "but I think I understand why."

"This is Corporal Underwood," Eric introduced the old soldier, his voice respectful. "Corporal, this is Molly... McClintock." With his hesitation, realization flared in his gray eyes.

She had almost become someone else. If she'd married, she wouldn't have been Molly McClintock anymore. She would have been Mrs. Towers. She would have changed her identity, which was probably why she'd accepted Josh's proposal in the first place. She'd wanted to be someone else.

"Pleased to meet you, miss," the old soldier greeted her with polished manners.

"The pleasure is mine, Corporal Underwood," Molly assured him.

The soldier shook Eric's arm. "Charm and beauty. She's a keeper."

"She's a friend," Eric quickly corrected the corporal.

Too quickly? But he was right. She was a friend. Just a friend—no matter what Abby, Brenna and Colleen claimed.

"So how are you feeling?" Eric asked, dropping to his haunches so he was eye to eye with the man in the wheelchair.

"Fine, Sarge," Corporal Underwood claimed, even though it was obvious he was not entirely fine. A tank on the back of his chair pumped oxygen through plastic tubing into his nose, but still each breath he drew rattled in his frail chest. Even so, as weak as he must have been, he'd probably have been too proud to use the chair if not for his missing leg.

"Now stop wasting your time with me, boy, and get in to see the major," the old man admonished him. "He's in his room."

Eric's jaw grew taut, and the skin around his scar puckered. "So he's not doing too well…"

The corporal shook his head. "I've seen a lot of soldiers come and go in this place. It probably won't be long now."

Molly's heart clenched in commiseration for Eric's pain and with a resurgence of her own pain. She still missed her dad. She didn't want Eric to experience that sense of loss but, then, he already had—when he was just a child. No wonder he understood her so well. Sometimes she thought he was the only one who understood; that was why she'd come to him.

As they walked down the hall, Eric's fingers closed around her hand and squeezed. "If this is hard for you…"

"It shouldn't be." But it was.

"This place is hard for a lot of people," he murmured,

his deep voice pitched low. "That's why they don't get many visitors."

"It's not that," she insisted. But she hadn't ever done well around sick people. That feeling of helplessness always overwhelmed her, paralyzing her. She had thought knowledge would have changed that, would have made her stronger, but it hadn't. Just volunteering at the hospital had been difficult for her, and yet her younger sister Colleen had been doing it regularly for years. Maybe Mom was right; Colleen was the stronger sister.

"Then you're thinking about your dad," he guessed. "I'm sorry."

"No. I'm thinking about you." About how he could have wound up here, and how he still might. When his uncle passed away he would have no family left. No one to take care of him when he got old…unless he got married and started a family of his own. Why did the thought bring her sadness rather than relief?

"I'm okay," he said. "I knew what to expect when Uncle Harold was diagnosed."

"Knowing and living through it are two different things," Molly said.

Immediately after they'd had that family meeting when her parents had told her and her siblings about her dad's cancer, she'd researched every aspect of the disease. She had hounded her father for every detail—which stage, how many milligrams of each medication, an explanation of every procedure. That was when Ronald McClintock had decided that she would become a doctor.

"Molly…"

She forced a bright smile. "You shouldn't have to do that alone, you know."

He squeezed her hand again. "I'm not alone."

"Not now. But I'm not staying."

The words slammed into Eric's gut. "Of course not." Why would she? Since graduation she had spent more time away at college than she had in Cloverville. She probably no longer considered it home.

"You need to find someone," she said, her eyes bright with the matchmaking gleam she'd inherited from her mother. "You're a great guy. You shouldn't be alone."

He stopped outside Uncle Harold's door. "I prefer to be single."

"No one *prefers* to be alone."

He couldn't argue with her now. Not here. Drawing a deep breath, he pushed open the door. A glass crashed, shattering against the jamb next to his head.

"Get out!" the major shrieked.

Ignoring the stinging he felt on his face, Eric rushed to his uncle's side. While the elderly man was often confused, he'd never been violent before. "Uncle Harold, it's me—Eric."

The old man's shoulders shook as he collapsed onto his bed, sobbing. "I'm sorry. I thought it was him—that nurse. He's trying to kill me."

"No, he's not," Eric assured his uncle. The paranoia and mood swings were worse than the confusion. "He's trying to help you."

If only someone could…

The old man blinked his gray eyes, and his gaze focused beyond Eric's shoulder. "It's that girl—the pretty little one you always followed around."

Eric turned his head to where Molly stood in the doorway, next to the broken glass. "Molly?"

"You're bleeding," she murmured as all color drained from her face. Then her legs folded, and like a rag doll she dropped to the floor.

Chapter Six

Eric's hand trembled against her face. "Molly? Molly?"

Her lashes fluttered then opened. "What happened?"

"You fainted."

She lifted her hand to his face. Then she pulled back, her fingers streaked red. "You're bleeding..."

Her brown eyes rolled back, and her lids closed again while her body went limp in his arms.

"You're bleeding, too," he whispered, wiping a drop of blood from her cheek. She'd fallen in the broken glass on the floor. His heart hammered against his ribs. He saw blood all the time, so much blood. But when it was hers it was different.

Was that why she had fainted? Because it was his blood? He half closed his eyes as he remembered a story Abby had told, of Molly passing out in the delivery room when Abby had given birth to her daughter, Lara. Maybe the sight of *anyone's* blood caused Molly to faint.

A smile tugged at his lips. Poor Molly. She was far too sensitive to be a doctor. The smile slipped away. Poor Molly. She couldn't do what she'd vowed to do when her dad died. She couldn't carry out her promise to her father.

Eric stroked her cheek and a shard of glass bit into his fingertip.

He had to get her cleaned up. "Molly? Come on, wake up…"

"Eric," she murmured his name, her lashes fluttering again.

Torn between concern for Molly and concern for his uncle, he turned toward the major. But the man appeared to be fine now, his paranoia and rage forgotten. "Uncle Harold?"

"Take care of the girl, boy." A grin brightened the major's face. "You've been taking care of her since you first came to live with me."

His uncle could remember twenty years ago and farther back, but minutes after Eric left he wouldn't remember his nephew's visit. Eric lifted Molly's limp body into his arms, forcing a smile for his great-uncle. "I'll be back soon."

"To take me home?"

Eric swallowed a sigh. "We'll see what the doctor says." About his uncle throwing things.

"That quack…"

Maybe the old man hadn't calmed down yet. Eric listened to his uncle rant as he carried Molly into the bathroom and propped her on the sink against the mirror. He gently washed the blood from her face, and she came around. Before she could faint again, he scrubbed the blood from his shallow scratches. "You okay?" he asked.

She nodded. "What about your uncle?"

"He doesn't usually throw things. I shouldn't have brought you here…." He closed his eyes and could see again the color draining from her face. "I'll take you back to Cloverville now."

"No. I want to stay."

He opened his eyes to meet her determined gaze. "Molly, you just passed out."

She wriggled down from the sink, brushing her body against his before she walked back into his uncle's room. In moments she had Uncle Harold laughing and smiling and acting like his old self. She not only entertained his uncle but all the other veterans who found an excuse to stop by the major's room to see what the ruckus was about.

Molly.

With her warmth and kindness, she drew people to her like flowers were drawn to sunshine. An hour later, as they walked back to his truck, clouds hung low in the afternoon sky. Eric opened the passenger door and helped her inside the cab.

"You've been quiet," she said as he slid behind the wheel.

"Uncle Harold would rather listen to you." The old man had truly enjoyed her visit; Eric hadn't seen him that happy in a long while.

Color tinged her delicate cheekbones. "I shouldn't have intruded."

Eric started the truck. "You better not apologize."

A giggle bubbled out of her. "Okay."

"Promise?" He steered his Ford out of the lot and pulled back onto the highway.

"You don't want my promise." Her breath shuddered out in a heavy sigh. "I tend to break my promises."

"Molly—"

"You can't argue with me, Eric. I broke my promise to you."

"What promise?" he asked.

"I promised to marry you," she reminded him.

He laughed. "We were in second grade. I can hardly expect you to keep *that* promise."

"My dad loved telling that story," she said, her voice soft with affection as she reminisced about her father, "about how when he came to pick me up from elementary school this little towheaded squirt walked up to him. And like an old-fashioned gentleman, you asked for his daughter's hand in marriage."

Eric laughed again. "That's not quite the way I remember it."

With a mist of tears in her eyes, she nodded. "Dad always admitted the truth, eventually, and confessed that you told him instead of asking him. You said, 'Molly's dad, I'm going to marry Molly.'"

"I was seven," he said.

"So you didn't know what you really wanted?"

He was afraid he knew more then than he did now. "I was seven," he repeated.

Disappointment tugged at Molly. "I'll be twenty-seven this fall, and I still don't know what I want," she admitted. How could she expect him to have known at seven?

"You're doing the right thing," he said, "taking time to figure that out before you face anyone."

"I'm not worried about facing anyone," she said. She knew her family and friends would forgive her and accept whatever decisions she made. She had to be able to accept herself—once she figured out who she really was.

"Not even your fiancé?"

"I talked to him the night before the wedding," she said, glancing down at the diamond on her hand. She should have given back Josh's ring then. Now, since she didn't have the jeweler's case, she felt as though she had to wear the ring to keep it safe until she could return it. And wearing the ring reminded her she'd made one mistake—she had to be careful not to make another.

Eric uttered an exaggerated gasp, as if scandalized by her admission. "I hope your mom doesn't know you broke tradition."

Molly shrugged. "Maybe she had reason to be superstitious."

"Obviously," he remarked, his mouth lifting in a faint grin.

Since he was driving, Molly resisted the urge to smack his arm. "Superstition wasn't why I didn't marry Josh."

"Cold feet?"

"Absolutely. And Josh knew that. He promised he would understand if I backed out. So I'm not worried about facing him." She had bigger problems.

"Understanding guy," Eric commented in a dry tone.

"I think he was having doubts himself, that he'd realized the same thing you and Abby and probably everyone else already had—that we'd rushed into it."

"Pretty irresponsible of the guy to rush into a relationship when he has two kids depending on him," Eric observed, his words full of disapproval.

"I think the boys might have been the reason he proposed so quickly."

"He wants a mother for his kids? What happened to theirs?"

"She was the irresponsible one. She abandoned them when the twins were babies." Guilt tugged at Molly. "And now I've abandoned them, too."

"Were they attached to you?"

"No." Molly sighed. "In fact I don't think they liked me very much."

Eric laughed. "I can't imagine *anyone* not liking you."

With Josh's busy schedule and hers, she hadn't spent much time with the boys. And the time she'd spent had been awkward, her efforts to charm them met with chilly silence. "I think they felt I was intruding. They were used to it being just guys."

"And you don't get much girlier than you."

This time she did smack his arm, heedless of his driving. "They need a woman in their lives." Eric should understand that. He'd needed one first after his parents had died, and then when his guardians had given him up to his great-uncle. "But maybe *I'm* not that woman."

The twins were another reason she'd gone out the window. If marrying Josh had turned out to be a mistake, another divorce would have been harder on the boys than a canceled wedding.

"Why did you accept his proposal?" Eric asked, his deep voice oddly gruff. "You two hadn't dated very long."

"From the first moment we met, we had a connection." Friendship that probably could have grown to love, although not a love as deep—and vulnerable—as the love her mother had felt for her father. Molly had thought, as Josh had, that a marriage based on friendship, rather than passion, would be stronger and safer. "Even though we hadn't known each other long, we thought we could make it work."

"Maybe you could have."

"It's too late now."

"I bet he'd take you back, if you explained that you just got cold feet."

Molly shook her head. Even if she wanted Josh back, she suspected—she *hoped*—he was busy falling for someone else. Brenna. She would make a much better wife, a much better mother for his sons. "It was more than cold feet," she insisted. "I'd realized I was making a mistake."

Josh deserved more. Her gaze slid to Eric's face, to his unmarred profile, as he concentrated on the highway. Maybe she deserved more, too.

"I don't know Towers personally, but I've heard all the gossip around the hospital," he admitted. "He's considered a great catch. Are you sure the mistake wasn't backing out of the wedding?"

She sighed. "Maybe it was." Maybe she would never find another guy as nice as Josh. But Eric drew her attention again. She had already found a guy as nice as Josh…when they were both seven.

"I'm going to pull into this gas station," Eric said.

Molly glanced toward the gauge. The tank was nearly full. "Okay."

Eric didn't park next to the pumps. He walked into the station instead. And took his time. When he finally rejoined her, with a pop bottle in each hand, Molly had slipped behind the wheel.

"You want to drive?" he asked.

"You took me where you go every Sunday. Now let me take you where I go." She held out her hand, palm up, for the keys.

Eric passed her a pop bottle instead. "Are you sure you can drive? You passed out cold a couple of times," he reminded her.

She nodded. "I'm fine." Now that all traces of blood were gone from his face. But she could imagine how he must have looked when he was hurt in the Middle East, when he'd nearly been killed. Maybe that was what she imagined every time she saw blood, because the sight of it hadn't bothered her much before he'd joined the Marines.

He hesitated another moment before pulling the keys from his pocket and dropping them into her hand. Then he walked around to the passenger side of the truck.

Molly waited until he buckled his seat belt before backing out and pulling onto the highway again. Silence settled between them as she drove back to Cloverville, the sound of the tires against the asphalt the only noise in the pickup cab.

When she pulled through the gates of Cloverville Cemetery, Eric broke his silence with a gasp of shock and concern. "You come here every Sunday?"

Her face flooded with color. "Only for the past few weeks. I hadn't been here for years before that. Guess that makes me a horrible daughter."

"Then I'm a horrible son. I haven't been to the cemetery in Chicago where my parents are buried…" He sighed. "In years. Uncle Harold used to take me on Memorial Day." They'd take the train down and make a weekend of it. He missed those times with his uncle more than he missed his parents, they'd been gone so long. Her dad had been gone a long time, too. "So why are coming now?" he asked.

"Because I need him now."

She'd been engaged, but she'd needed her father more than her fiancé?

"You probably think I'm crazy, huh?" she continued. "I know he's not really here. But…"

Eric opened the truck door. "But you feel close to him here."

Her breath shuddered out. "I never should have doubted that you would understand."

He crossed around the front of the truck, before she

could open her door, and helped her out. She wore a dress today, but this was a short one with a flouncy hem that fluttered around her knees and rode up her slim thighs when she'd been sitting in the truck. When he'd been behind the wheel, he had needed all his concentration not to drive into the ditch. After clearing his throat, he said, "You know your dad would understand, too."

"What? My coming here?" She shook her head. "Actually, he would probably be mad."

Thinking of her father brought a bittersweet grin to Eric's lips. Mr. McClintock had been such a great guy. "Yeah, he probably would."

Molly smiled, too, and her eyes brightened. "Can't you just hear him telling me that I have better things to do than spend my time here?"

He had always told Eric and the rest of Molly's friends that they had better things to do whenever they visited him when he'd been sick. He had been sick for so long. Eric closed his hand around Molly's as they walked toward her father's grave. "He'd probably be mad about more than your visits."

Molly nodded. "He was always so big on honor—and integrity. He would be mad that I ran out on my wedding, that I backed out on a commitment I made."

Eric shook his head. "No, he wouldn't. He would understand."

"I hope so…"

"And not just about your wedding. He'd understand about your dropping out of med school."

She stared at the granite stone that designated Ronald James McClintock, beloved husband and father. Her voice cracked with emotion as she admitted, "I broke my promise to him, Eric."

"He wouldn't care," Eric insisted, his heart hurting with the pain darkening her brown eyes. "In fact he'd be mad that you were forcing yourself to do something you didn't enjoy. Your father only wanted one thing for you."

"For me to become a doctor."

Shaking his head, he insisted, "Happiness. That's all he wanted."

She expelled a wistful sigh. "I wish…"

"C'mon, Molly, you know I'm right." He squeezed her hand.

But she pulled away. "No. He wanted more for me than just happiness."

"*Just* happiness?" Did she have any idea how difficult happiness was to find? So difficult that Eric had decided a while ago to just give up.

"He wanted me to help people," she explained, "because no one had been able to help him."

"That's what *you* wanted, Molly."

"He was my dad, Eric. I know what he wanted," she insisted, bristling with stubborn pride. "And I let him down. I disappointed him."

Eric closed his hands around her shoulders and tried to pull her close. But Molly's body remained tense with guilt and pain. That was why she'd been coming to visit her father the past few weeks, probably in the hopes that he would somehow release her from the promise she had made. "So what are you going to do? Go back to medical school, even though you hate it?"

"That's what I should do." She drew in a breath, as if bracing herself for something horrible. "That's what I need to do."

"If you hate it, going back, making yourself miserable... *That* would be crazy."

"You're a fine one to talk," she accused him, her eyes dark with anger. "You joined the Marines to please your uncle, to repay him for taking you in when you—"

"When I had no place else to go? Yeah, I owe my uncle," he admitted. "But that's not why I joined the Marines. It was something inside." He pressed a fist to his heart. "Something I felt I had to do because *I* wanted to enlist, not because someone else wanted me to."

She reached up and brushed her fingers across his cheek. "And look what it got you. You shouldn't have joined. You should have listened to me that night."

"The night we swore we'd never mention again?" he asked. "*That* night?"

Her delicate throat moved as she swallowed, and her skin reddened. "That night. I can't believe I..."

"Don't worry," he said, "I never told anyone. You have no reason to be embarrassed."

"Eric..."

"But we're not talking about that night and we're not talking about me," he reminded her. He hated talking about himself. "We're talking about *you,* about what you're going to do."

"I don't know what I'm going to do. Just yesterday I was in the brides' room at church, getting ready to marry a man I'd dated only a few months," she admitted. "I'm not rushing into any more decisions. I'm going to take my time."

"And this time base your decisions on what *you* want," he advised her, trying to be the supportive friend she expected him to be. "Not what you think someone else wants for you."

"I can't be like you, Eric. I can't *not* care about what

other people, about what people I care about, want." Accusation burned brightly in her eyes. "Even though I begged you not to go, you still left me when I needed you most."

"You were leaving, too," he reminded her as guilt gnawed at him. For years, he'd beat himself up for making her cry, for hurting her. He continued, "In just a couple of months, you and Brenna were going off to college. Abby had already taken off. It wasn't fair of you to ask me to stay when you weren't staying."

She lifted her arms and gestured at the tombstones around them. "I didn't want you to wind up here. I didn't want to lose you like I'd just lost my dad."

"I know." He reached out, pulling her into his arms and close against his heart. "But you didn't lose me."

She stepped back and shook her head. "But I did. You're not the man who left Cloverville."

"A boy left." And came back a man.

"I miss the boy," she said wistfully.

"Everyone has to grow up sometime, Molly. You're too old for anyone else to make your decisions. Not your father or me or Josh Towers."

She turned toward Mr. McClintock's tombstone, her thick lashes blinking as if she fought back tears. "I know."

"Molly…"

"Please, just leave me here," she said. "I want to be alone for a while."

Everyone else had respected her wish for time alone. Everyone except him. He nodded, then turned, and once again he left her alone with her pain.

MOLLY HELD HER BREATH waiting for the crank of the truck engine, but it never came. She glanced back toward the red

Ford, to see if Eric was waiting for her. But he was gone. Walking to town with his limp? Even as slight as it was, it must bother him. More guilt pressed on her heart, weighing it down even more.

"I'm sorry," she whispered, even though he had to be out of earshot since she couldn't see him. She had done nothing but disrupt his life since she'd showed up at his door. She couldn't stay with him, not while she got her head together. That would probably take entirely too long.

"Here you go," murmured a feminine voice as an elderly woman stooped and placed flowers on Molly's dad's grave. More flowers bobbed on her wide-brimmed hat as she straightened up. "I see that you didn't bring any flowers this Sunday."

"I didn't think I'd be here," Molly admitted.

Mrs. Hild's gently wrinkled face lifted in a smile. "You were supposed to be on your honeymoon."

Molly sighed. "Yes."

"Instead, you're here."

Because she hadn't loved Josh, she would rather be here than on a honeymoon with him. She'd been crazy—and cowardly—to think she could marry without love.

"I passed Eric on his way out," Mrs. Hild said. "He said you wanted to be alone."

Yet the old woman persisted in talking to her. Molly sighed again, and her irritation eased with her breath. Mrs. Hild, despite her reputation as the town gossip, was really a very sweet woman. "I appreciate the flowers. I'm sure my father would, too."

"But you're not alone," Mrs. Hild continued as if Molly hadn't spoken. "You're with your father."

She wished he were here—in more than spirit—with her.

Mrs. Hild entwined her gnarled fingers as she stared across the cemetery, toward a grave nearly covered with a profusion of fresh roses. "I come here every chance I get so I can be with Ernest."

"You still miss him a lot?"

"I miss him." The widow sighed. "And I miss what we could have had."

"He's been gone a long time." Molly couldn't even remember Mr. Hild. "You still miss him?"

The older woman nodded and sent the flowers on her hat brim bobbing again. "Every day."

"I'm sorry." Molly was sorry she had ever considered getting married.

"I'm sorry, too," the older woman said with a heavy sigh. "I wasted so much time."

"I don't understand. If you feel closer to Ernest here, then you're not wasting your time visiting." Molly reached out, wrapping her fingers around Mrs. Hild's clasped hands.

"Oh, no, I'm not talking about visiting his grave," the widow insisted. "I wasted *our* time before he died."

"How?"

"Ernest asked me three times to marry him before I finally got smart and accepted. I wasted so much time. Years we were apart. I kept telling him that I wasn't ready to settle down." Tears sparkled in the other woman's faded blue eyes. "The truth was that I wasn't ready to *settle*."

Molly squeezed her companion's hands, offering silent comfort. She recognized and understood her guilt.

"He was my high-school sweetheart, you know." Mrs. Hild laughed. "Heck, elementary school. We grew up together. I didn't think it was really love. I thought it was convenience. So when he proposed after graduation, I turned him down. I wanted to see if there was more out there, if there was *someone* better out there. So, like Abby Hamilton, I left Cloverville for a while. But I was wrong. There was no one better—period. Ernest was the best. And I wasted so much of the time we could have had together looking for something I'd had all along with him—true love."

"But at least you had true love," Molly pointed out. "That's more than most people can say."

Mrs. Hild nodded, and a tear slipped from her eye and trailed down her weathered cheek. "I know. But I would have had it longer, if I hadn't been afraid."

Fear tightened Molly's stomach as the elderly widow warned her, "Don't be afraid, Molly. Don't waste your happiness."

Chapter Seven

The clouds still hung low and dark in the sky, and the distant rumble of thunder threatened a storm. Perfect time for a Sunday stroll, Eric chided himself. But he hadn't wanted to wait in the truck for Molly. She wasn't the only one who needed time alone.

The reprieve in the gas station hadn't been long enough—not to erase from his mind her talk of Dr. Towers and their instant connection. Of course she would have fallen for Josh easier than for him. She'd known Eric for nearly twenty years and hadn't *ever* fallen for him.

His steps slowed as he neared the gated entrance to Cloverville Park. Why did they even bother with the gates, when he could never remember them being closed? But no one closed gates or locked doors in Cloverville. The town was safe, unlike those places Eric had been in the Marines, but still bad things happened here—like Mr. McClintock dying. And Colonel Clover's "accident."

Eric walked into the park and kept walking until the distorted shadow of Colonel Clover fell across his face. He stared up at the bent and broken statue of the town founder. Eight years ago someone had driven through the park and smashed into the statue, bending and breaking the old metal. Abby Hamilton had taken the blame; it had been her car, after all, and no one in town doubted she'd been the driver. Except for her friends.

They'd all known she hadn't been behind the wheel; Molly's younger sister had been. But Colleen had been so miserable and so obviously guilty that no one had had the heart to call her on it. They hadn't wanted her to feel any worse. And Abby had always planned on leaving Cloverville anyway. She hadn't needed an excuse, but Colleen had given her another, quite convenient one.

Eric winked at the colonel, silently thanking him for keeping Colleen's secret, too. Colonel Clover, more than anything or anyone else in town, made Eric feel at home. Next to the broken statue, he didn't feel so damaged.

"Eric South!"

He jumped at the booming voice. Two years out of the Corps, and his reflexes were a little dull. He should have noticed he wasn't alone in the park. "Hey, Pop. Mama." He nodded at Brenna Kelly's parents.

"So, I hear you have a houseguest," Mama said with a teasing smile. Her dark eyes bright with amusement, she patted her hair. It had been white as long as he could remember, even though he'd heard it was once as red as her daughter's.

He glanced at Pop. Eric hadn't confirmed where Molly was staying, but obviously the old man had his suspicions. "I never said I had a houseguest."

Pop put a hand on his shoulder. "You didn't have to, boy."

God, did everyone know how he felt about Molly? That he could never tell her no? Except that once…

"Women talk," Pop added.

"Mary McClintock called me this morning," Mama explained. The two women had always been close friends.

"You didn't tell Brenna?" he asked, as protective of Molly as he'd always been. "Or the groom?"

Mama shook her head. "No, Mary and I agreed that everyone would be better off if we let Molly come home under her own steam."

Tensing with alarm, Eric's hands fisted. "Would Dr. Towers be the type to drag her home if he knew where she was?" Maybe the women on staff at the hospital were wrong about him.

"Oh, goodness, no," Mama defended the groom, fluttering a hand against her chest in one of her many dramatic mannerisms.

Eric had always found the Kellys so entertaining— until today.

"Josh would never pressure Molly," Pop assured him with respect for the surgeon.

"He wouldn't have to," Mama said with a wink. "I understand why she accepted his proposal. The man is beautiful, outside and in." She shook her head. "I just can't understand why she jilted him."

Pop nodded toward the playground, to the young dark-haired twins twirling on the merry-go-round. "Maybe it all seemed like too much."

"They're such sweet boys. You should meet them, Eric," Mama said with all the pride of a grandparent.

But Brenna hadn't made them grandparents. Yet. Eric figured his redheaded friend planned to—eventually. When they were kids, she had appointed herself mother of their group. He knew she would be a natural when she started a family of her own.

He glanced over at the merry-go-round and the kids who were miniatures of their good-looking father. Last night Brenna had seemed interested in the doctor and he in her. But Eric might have imagined the sparks between the maid of honor and the groom. He might have just been hoping that the doctor was interested in a woman other than Molly.

With her generous heart and loving nature, Molly would make a wonderful mother, too. She would have been a great stepmother for the Towers twins, once they'd given her a chance. She still might, if she decided she wanted to marry Towers after all.

"I really can't meet the kids right now," he said. "I have to get back…"

To nothing. He had no idea if Molly had left the cemetery, or if she had… If she intended to return to his house or find another less complicated place to stay, like her home. Or maybe she'd guilted herself into returning to medical school. She wouldn't need much time to pack her things in the car he'd stowed in his barn. She might already be gone.

"They're really neat boys," Pop said, gesturing toward the twins.

"I'm sure they are," Eric agreed. "But me and kids…" He stroked a finger over his cheek and forced a chuckle. "We tend to give each other nightmares."

Pop laughed and slapped a hand against his shoulder again. "You're such a kidder."

But Eric wasn't kidding. He really did give children nightmares. The last woman he'd dated had had a couple of kids, and she'd shared that with him as her reason for breaking up. She hadn't meant to be cruel to Eric; she'd just wanted to be a good mother. He had respected her honesty. And he hadn't really cared enough to take it personally.

"We did promise to take the twins for ice cream," Mrs. Kelly reminded her husband.

They left Eric with a few more words of praise for the boys—and for the man they would obviously have liked for a son-in-law. Was everyone in Cloverville a matchmaker? If Molly changed her mind about marrying Towers, she might have competition now.

Hell, she was Molly. Beautiful and smart. So was Brenna, but Molly had something extra—something that made her so special that a man could never get her completely out of his head or his heart.

He waved to the Kellys and the twins as they rushed out of the park and headed off toward town. He stood a moment longer, in the shadow of the colonel until another man entered the park, the fair-haired best man. Along with a rolled-up blanket under his arm, Dr. Jameson carried a picnic basket. Before the other man noticed him, Eric slipped through the gates. But he waited—not long—to see who showed up.

Colleen. She didn't rush toward the man who must have been waiting for *her.* Instead she lingered outside, watching him. Although she hadn't been hurt as badly as Colonel Clover in the accident all those years ago, she still bore scars from losing her father—and herself for a while—in her adolescence. She'd been hurt enough to remain cautious.

Mrs. McClintock had been right to assure her oldest daughter that she didn't need to worry about her younger sister. Knowing Colleen could take care of herself—even though she might have yet to realize it—Eric turned away from the park and headed toward the small cabin he'd called home for almost twenty years.

Eric understood caution. First he'd lost his folks, and

then he'd lost his guardians. Except for Uncle Harold, people had a habit of letting him down—of letting him go. Then he'd entered the Marines and he'd learned that he needed to be cautious in every aspect of his life.

Never more so than now—with Molly in residence.

Unless she'd already left.

"YOU CAME HOME." Relief eased the tight knot in Molly's stomach. She dropped the book she'd been trying unsuccessfully to read onto the couch.

His voice tinged with irony, he replied, "I do live here, you know."

"I thought maybe you took me at my word. And you went to Grand Rapids to stay with your friend."

He pressed the door shut with his back and rubbed his hip. With a rueful half grin, he admitted, "I'm not sure I could have managed the walk to Grand Rapids."

"Are you all right?" Concern propelled her from the couch to his side.

"I'm fine. I'm just getting old."

"You're only twenty-six." Same as her. But those years in the Marines had aged him. Heck, even when they'd been kids he'd seemed older, despite his small size. Of course by the age of seven, he'd already suffered way too much loss.

"You should have taken your truck," she said. A rumble of distant thunder reinforced her reprimand. "I was worried about you."

"I needed to walk." He eased away from the door—and her—and limped toward the kitchen. "My physical therapist tells me I don't walk enough."

"I was worried that you'd get caught in a storm." And

so she'd searched for him, driving his truck with a cap pulled low over her face so that no one would recognize her. But with dark clouds threatening, not many people had been out walking the sidewalks of Cloverville. Only Eric.

"You don't need to worry about me." He waved off her concern as he jerked open the door to his copper-toned refrigerator.

"But I do." She had gotten used to worrying about him. Even after his return from the Marines, she hadn't been able to break the habit.

"You're wasting your time," he remarked as he poured himself a glass of iced tea. Then he turned toward Molly, lifting the pitcher in a silent question.

She shook her head. "I don't want anything to drink. But I can't deny that I might have wasted my time."

"Of course you have. There's no reason to worry about me," he insisted. "I'm fine."

"I'm not talking about you." Because she wasn't likely to stop worrying about him yet. "I think I might have wasted my time in medical school." And those years in premed classes at college when she would have rather taken liberal-arts courses. So many years wasted, if she changed her mind. How could she give up now, after promising her dad, after working so hard?

How could she throw away so many years of her life?

"Molly…"

"You knew that, too, that I wasn't cut out for medical school. Just like you knew I was jumping into marriage with Josh. Why didn't you say something before you left?" She had cared enough then to try and stop him from entering the Marines. Why hadn't he cared enough about her to stop her from wasting her life?

"You know why," he said as he opened the sliders and stepped onto the deck. He stared out over the lake.

Even though she knew he didn't want to talk to her, she followed him. "Are you mad at me?" she asked, grasping his arm in her hands. The hair on his forearms tickled her palms.

He turned back toward her and sighed. "No."

"But I was kind of a bitch at the cemetery," she admitted, her voice rasping with regret. "I had no right to lash out at you just because I'm confused."

"You weren't bitchy, you were being stubborn. In other words—you were being you." He sighed. "When you get something in your head, you don't listen."

"So that's why you've never told me all the mistakes I've been making?"

"I told you once," he reminded her. "Just once…"

Molly's face heated as she remembered when—in his bedroom eight years before. She dropped his arm and knotted her hands together. "I—I—uh…" She swallowed her nerves. "I know I brought it up at the cemetery. But we need to go back to forgetting that night ever happened."

Eric turned toward the lake again and sighed. "If only I could."

"I ruined our friendship, didn't I? That night… Just like I always thought it would."

He lifted brows above eyes as dark a gray as the overhead clouds. *"It?"*

Her pulse quickened to a crazy rhythm. "We're not talking about it," she insisted.

"But we're both thinking about it now."

"I should go. I made another mistake coming here." She turned toward the patio doors, but when she reached for the handle, a strong hand closed over hers.

"You didn't ruin anything that night, Molly."

A smile twitched at her lips. "Liar."

Eric uttered a deep, throaty chuckle. "I'm not lying. That happened a long time ago, and we're still friends."

"That's why I should leave now." She sighed. "Because just give me a chance, and I will screw things up. I've made a pretty big mess of my life lately. So I strongly suggest that you save yourself."

His hand slid off hers. "Okay, get out."

"Eric!"

"I'm kidding, Molly," he said. "I really don't want you to go."

Her heart lifting with relief because he didn't actually want her to leave, she teasingly accused him, "Masochist."

He expelled a ragged sigh. "Tell me about it!"

"So you're not mad at me?"

"Over what?" he asked. "The cemetery, or what we promised to forget?"

"The cemetery," she interjected. "You were being so supportive, which is all you've been since I showed up at your door." That night really hadn't hurt their friendship. "And I thanked you by being all bitch—"

"Stubborn," he interrupted her.

"But you wound up walking home. I'm sorry."

"What did I say about apologizing?"

"To quit it," she repeated. As if possessed by a mischievous imp, she teased, "So I'll quit *saying* I'm sorry. And *show* you how sorry I am."

Eric's dark blond brows furrowed. "What are you…"

She rose on tiptoes and threw an arm around his neck, pulling his head down for a kiss. As she pressed her lips to his, she realized she'd done it again.

She'd made another mistake. Not because she kissed him, but because she didn't want the kiss to end. With her free hand she grasped his T-shirt, pulling him closer as she moved her mouth over his.

Eric's lips parted on a groan, and he deepened the kiss. His tongue slipped inside her mouth, hot and hungry, while his hands moved over her, tangling in her hair, running down her back and clutching her hips.

Molly's knees weakened as the heat of desire flooded her body. She trembled in his arms, wanting more. "Eric?"

Chapter Eight

"Eric?"

His body tense and throbbing, Eric jerked back until Molly's arms fell to her sides and her thick lashes blinked open.

"Eric?"

"Uh-uh. It's probably not a good idea to *show* me you're sorry, either," he said, his voice gruff, even though he'd tried for light and friendly. He didn't want to have to assure her again that she hadn't ruined anything.

Color rushed to Molly's face, painting her cheekbones dark rose. "I didn't mean... I wasn't trying..."

"I know." She didn't have to try. That had always been the problem with resisting his attraction to her.

Her dark eyes wide, she stammered, "I—I don't want you to think..."

What? Before he could actually work up the nerve to ask, someone else called his name from around the side of the cabin. "Eric?"

"Rory?" Molly mouthed at him.

He nodded and glanced down at his watch. "Yeah, I'm back here."

Molly shoved his chest—probably in protest of his call to Rory—but the memory of her hands on his body, her lips pressed to his continued to flit through his mind, reminding him of what he'd just stopped. Molly turned and fled into the house just as her teenage brother rounded the corner of the cabin.

"Hey, man!" Rory said.

"Hey," Eric called back. "I wasn't sure you'd make it today." But he was damned glad he had.

"Why wouldn't I?" Rory asked, his brown eyes narrowing with suspicion.

Clearly his mother hadn't told him where Molly was, or at least she hadn't told him to leave his oldest sister alone.

"Uh, it looks like rain." Eric pointed to the ominous sky.

"You always say the fish bite more when it looks like it's gonna rain," Rory reminded him.

"Yeah, I'm sure the fish are biting," Eric said, hiding his surprise that the kid had actually paid attention to him. "But I didn't think you'd make our standing fishing appointment, since you've got houseguests."

"From what I hear, you got a houseguest, too," Rory replied in a loud voice. He glanced toward the partially open slider and grinned. "Hey, Mol! You can stop hiding. I know you're here—come out!"

Eric wouldn't lie to Rory, not even for Molly, but he tried steering him toward the dock. "C'mon, let's get out on the lake before this storm actually hits."

"So you're not gonna try and tell me she's not here?" Rory asked, his eyes wide.

Eric couldn't. When he'd caught the kid drinking in the park with the Hendrix boys, he and Rory had made a pact to never lie to each other.

"I'm here," Molly admitted as she stepped back onto the deck. "But you shouldn't be."

"Why not? You want Eric all to yourself?" the teenager teased.

Molly's face flushed again and she shoved her brother this time. "No. If people know you've stopped over here, they're going to ask you if you saw me."

"So?" Rory retorted. "I'll lie for you."

"Really?" his older sister asked, as if stunned by her sibling's loyalty.

"Sure," he agreed, and then qualified his answer. "For the right price."

"You little twerp."

"Careful. Insults drive up my fee," he taunted. "Now I'll need more incentive to keep your secret."

"Maybe I should just call Mom," his big sister threatened.

The mischievous glint flickered out of Rory's eyes. "Uh, you don't need to do that."

"You're not even supposed to be here, are you?" she guessed. "Mom told you not to come?"

"She used some excuse about needing me to entertain Lara. But it was a pretty lame excuse," Rory commented. "That's when I figured you were here."

The teenager was smart. Too smart to be getting himself into so much trouble.

"And you had to rush over to hassle me?" she asked.

Her little brother grinned. "It was too good to pass up."

"You're enjoying this?"

"Smart, perfect Molly messing up?" He whistled. "Oh, yeah, I'm enjoying it. Maybe I'll finally stop getting told by Mom, Clayton and every teacher at school that I should try to be like my oldest sister."

Molly protested, "Rory, I think you're exaggerating."

"Looks like they're the ones who've been exaggerating. You're not so perfect after all."

"Hey, you two. Seriously, it looks like the storm's moving closer," Eric pointed toward the sky. Actually it had looked the same most of the afternoon, but Eric didn't want to be in the middle of a family fight. Especially since he cared about both siblings. "You should probably get home before you get stuck here. I'll give you a ride in the truck."

Rory shook his curly head. "That's all right. I rode my moped over."

"I can throw it in the back of the truck." And get some much-needed time and distance away from Molly.

"No, it's okay, really. You drive so slow, old man, that I can get home just as fast on my own," he teased, mischief glinting in his dark eyes again.

"Rory, mind your manners," his sister admonished him.

"It's just Eric, Mol."

It's just Eric. Was that how she saw him? Eric swallowed a sigh, knowing that it probably was.

"He's not an old man," Molly defended him.

"Yeah, he's not as old as your groom, that's for sure."

Eric suppressed the chuckle that was burning his throat. Towers was probably only five or six years older than he was.

"Is that why you left the guy at the altar, Mol?"

"Rory!" Outrage flashed in her eyes and she reached for her younger brother.

Lifting his hands as if to fend her off, he stepped back. "Don't get violent," he joked. "I'll get out of here."

"You better head home before Mom notices you're gone. She probably really needs your help with Lara."

He shrugged. "Lara's pretty cool for a little girl."

"You be cool," Molly warned him. "And don't you dare tell anyone you saw me."

"We'll negotiate my price later," Rory teased as he headed around the corner of the cabin. Then, over his shoulder, he tossed out his best Arnold Schwarzenegger impersonation, "I'll be baaaack."

Eric twisted his mouth, biting the corner of his lip to stop himself from grinning at the kid's antics.

"He's such a little creep," Molly said, huffing in an agitated breath of outrage.

"He's a teenager." Rory was wild and reckless, Eric thought, but not wanting to add to Molly's worries, he kept that to himself.

"He's a twerp." She drew in another breath as if to calm herself. "You really have a standing fishing date with him?"

"Appointment," Eric corrected her. "We're guys—we don't *date*. But we do fish every Sunday afternoon."

"Why?"

Eric shrugged. "I figured he could use another guy in his life."

"He has Clayton. You know how my older brother loves assuming responsibility for everyone around him," she said with a faint trace of bitterness.

Eric nodded. "I figured he could use someone a little less, uh…"

"Rigid?" she supplied.

"Yeah, a little less rigid than Clayton." The oldest McClintock sibling made Eric's boot-camp drill sergeant look easygoing by comparison.

Molly reached out, brushing her fingers over his forearm. "That's really sweet of you to do that, to be there for him."

He would have liked to be there for her—as more than

a friend. But the diamond of her engagement ring glinted on her hand, reminding him that she still officially belonged to another man.

"Well, I think I get more out of our Sunday afternoons than he does," he admitted. "Rory always makes me laugh." Something Eric hadn't done much of since he'd been a kid himself. Shrugging off her hand, he turned toward the lake, to his fishing boat roped to the dock. "I shouldn't have sent him home."

"Thanks for doing that," she said, her voice full of gratitude. "Of course it's probably too late, since he saw me here."

"He'll keep quiet," Eric assured her.

"You sound confident." Her dark eyes narrowed. "What do you have on him?"

"I think I'll go out on the water, anyway," he said, ignoring her question as he continued to stare at his boat, bobbing on the wind-driven waves.

"You told him it looks like it's going to storm," she reminded him.

"The clouds are moving off. I doubt I'd even get wet," he predicted. Not that he couldn't use a dip in the cool lake water. His body still ached from their kiss. He definitely needed a cold shower.

"Then, I'll go out with you." She invited herself. "It's been a long time since I went fishing."

"Molly…"

Molly smiled, hearing the groan in his voice. But it wasn't like when he'd groaned earlier, when she'd kissed him. "C'mon, Eric, I want to go with you."

She wanted to do more than fish with him, but she had to settle for fishing. She still wore one man's ring, and she shouldn't be kissing—or doing anything else—with another one. Not even *after* she returned the ring. She couldn't jump into anything else, career- or relationship-wise. She wore the ring not only to protect it, but also to protect herself from making another impulsive decision.

"I'm not throwing back the fish like you used to make me do," he warned as he headed toward the dock.

Molly rushed after him. "Don't we need poles? Bait?"

"You want to dig for night crawlers?" he asked.

She shuddered. "No."

"I have tackle boxes and poles in the boat," he explained as he stepped off the dock, his long legs easily managing the distance between deck boards and boat.

Molly stopped on the edge of the dock. Wedge sandals and a short dress weren't the most practical clothes for fishing. But she didn't trust Eric to wait for her if she went back to the house to change.

Eric sighed—a sigh that sounded suspiciously long-suffering—then reached out for her. "Take my hand."

"Always." She entwined her fingers with his and stepped off the dock. As she joined him, the boat rocked beneath her feet, and she fell against Eric's lean, hard body. Her breath escaped in a gasp.

"Careful," he cautioned, helping her settle onto one of the bench seats.

She wasn't going to be too stubborn to take his advice this time—both in the boat and her life. From now on she would be careful, so no more kissing him. "You'll still bait my hook?" she asked.

Eric sighed again. "I wonder if I can catch Rory," he mused aloud.

Molly smacked his arm, rocking the boat again. "So you'd prefer him to me?"

"I don't have to bait *his* hook," Eric said as he untied the boat.

"He probably baits yours," she accused. "What do you have on him?"

"What do you mean?"

"You're not worried about him telling anyone that I'm staying here," she reminded him. Given how well he knew her, he should have known better than to try to distract her with a change of subject. Even she was aware that her single-mindedness was a Cloverville legend. "You have some dirt on my little brother. Spill it."

Eric shook his head, and the light breeze ruffled his dark blond hair. "Nope. I don't tell secrets."

"So you do have dirt on Rory." She studied Eric through narrowed eyes, but he didn't squirm beneath her scrutiny. Instead he ignored her and rowed to the middle of the lake. But Molly couldn't ignore him or the way his biceps strained the sleeves of his T-shirt, flexing with each push of his hands against the oars.

Eric's gaze met hers, his eyes darkening as he caught her staring. Molly pulled her attention from *him,* glancing around at the lake. With only the single dock, and trees rimming its banks except for the cabin, the lake had an undisturbed beauty. Water slapped against the boat, rippling away in undulating currents.

She pulled her mind from Eric, as well, refocusing on her brother. "So Rory's been getting into trouble," she surmised.

"You'll have to ask him." Eric handed her a fishing pole. "Here, I baited it."

Understanding that he wanted some peace for fishing, Molly managed to keep quiet. Until something tugged on her line, and then she shrieked.

"Reel it in," Eric advised.

Molly's fingers fumbled with the reel, trying to turn it. "I—I can't, the reel's rusty."

"You're rusty. When's the last time you went fishing?" he asked.

"With you…"

Eric set aside his own pole and moved behind her so that he spooned her body, his arms around her, his fingers over hers as he helped her crank the reel. Gripping the pole, Molly leaned back, pressing against his chest. Her breath stuck in her lungs as every nerve ending tingled.

Then Eric jerked the pole out of the water and the cold, wet fish, wriggling on the line, slapped against Molly. Startled, she shrieked again and jumped up, knocking Eric back. The boat rocked and then tipped, toppling the poles, the fish, the tackle boxes and them into the lake.

"GOOD THING YOUR MOM brought leftovers," Eric said as Molly carried a tray outside, to where he'd started a bonfire on the sandy beach. "Since you got your way, and the fish got released."

"Catch and release," Molly murmured. "That's my motto. With fish and men."

As she set the tray on the sand, he touched the diamond on her finger and reminded her. "You haven't released Towers yet."

"Oh, this?" She glanced down at the ring as if she'd forgotten she still wore it. Seeing as how she'd kissed Eric not once but twice, maybe she had forgotten.

If only he could.

When they'd stumbled ashore, her wet dress had been nearly transparent, hugging every sweet curve of her body.

He'd used all his willpower to keep himself from pulling her down onto the sand and burying himself inside her.

"I'm going to give it back to him," she insisted.

Holding his breath, he asked, "When?"

She dropped down beside him on the blanket he'd laid atop the sand, and sighed. "I don't know."

"Because then you'll have to talk to him?" Jealousy gripped him.

"Because then I'll have no reason to stay here."

His heart clenched. "You want to stay here?"

"I—I need to sort some things out yet. It's only been a day," she reminded him.

Was it just yesterday that she was supposed to have married another man?

"Seems longer," he remarked.

She jammed an elbow into his ribs, and he flopped back onto the blanket, groaning as if in agony. She immediately rolled to her side and leaned over him, her face tight with concern. "Did I hurt you? I'm so—"

Eric pressed his fingers against her lips. "I'm goofing around. Your bony elbow didn't hurt me."

She glared at him. "I really miss the days when you were smaller than me."

"Second grade."

"Through the end of our sophomore year."

"I was small," he admitted, "but not smaller than you. You're tiny." But perfect.

"I'm petite," she corrected him. "Like my mom."

"I think you're even shorter than your mom," he observed.

With disgust, she said, "Rory calls me the runt of the litter now, even though he's the youngest."

"Well, you are the smallest McClintock…"

"But I could always take you," she reminisced.

Eric grinned. "Only because I let you."

"Bullshit."

"Oh, potty mouth," he admonished her, as if they were still in second grade. "Do I have to tell your mama that you swore?"

"You wouldn't dare," she threatened, leaning over him so that their faces nearly bumped. She drew in a breath and straightened up, wrapping her arms around her knees. Clearly there were some things she didn't dare—like getting within kissing distance of him again. "You're the secrets keeper."

"Yeah, that's me."

"Seriously," she persisted, "tell me what's up with Rory."

He leaned closer to the fire. "You dry yet?" He knew that only her hair was wet, damp tendrils hanging down her back, since she had changed into her boxer shorts and cami when she'd gone inside the house for food. One of the spaghetti straps of the tank top cut across the spine of the open book that was tattooed on her shoulder blade. He curled his fingers into his palm, so he wouldn't reach up to trace the outline of it.

"Eric!" she said, her voice sharp with irritation because he wouldn't satisfy her curiosity about her little brother.

He shook his head. "Since you're so tough, you're going to have to beat it out of me."

"Don't tempt me."

His skin heated at the intensity of her gaze, as she ran it like a caress over his body. He'd changed into dry jeans and a short-sleeved shirt that he'd left unbuttoned. "Molly…"

She launched herself at him, knocking him back onto the blanket with such force that sand wafted up from beneath it. She leaned across his bare chest and lifted his arms over his head, her hands splayed across his biceps, pinning him down. Then she swung her leg across his. "Say uncle."

"Uncle…"

She *tsk*ed as if she was disappointed in him. "What kind of Marine are you? To give up without a fight?"

A muscle jumped in his jaw. She was right—he had never given up without a fight. But the only thing he wanted to fight with Molly was his attraction to her. And with her body, so soft and curvy, pressed close to his, he couldn't fight anything.

ONE MINUTE MOLLY was lying across him and the next Eric had flipped her on her back and pressed her into the sand with his body. Hot and hard against hers.

Her breath whooshed out of her lungs. She lifted her hands to his shoulders, but not to push him away. She wanted to pull him closer. But his hands wrapped around her wrists, lifting her arms over her head as he pinned her to the sand.

Molly's back arched, her breasts pushing against his solid chest. His heart beat fast and furious, in perfect rhythm with hers. "Eric…"

He leaned closer, his lips just a breath away from hers, he murmured, "Say uncle."

She bucked against him, trying to dislodge him. But he straddled her, so her hips pressed against his. As if there were no clothes between them, as if they were making love…

Eric closed his eyes and uttered a tortured groan. "Say uncle, Molly."

She bucked again, pressing her breasts and hips against

him. This time she groaned, her body aching with an emptiness she suspected only Eric could fill.

He settled more of his weight onto her, so that not even a breath separated his chest from hers. So that his erection, straining against the fly of his jeans, pressed against her.

So that he closed that fraction of space between his mouth and hers and their lips met.

Chapter Nine

As the door rattled in reaction to a pounding fist, Eric tensed. It was Towers. It had to be. Someone had told him where to find his runaway bride. And he had come to claim her—just as Eric would have if she'd been his.

But she had never really been his. Not even last night.

Fists clenched and ready for a fight, he drew open the door…to Mrs. McClintock. "Good morning," he murmured.

"Good afternoon," Mrs. Mick corrected him, patting his cheek as she passed through the doorway. "This is two days in a row I've had to wake you two. What are you doing? Staying up all night?"

"Mom!"

Eric turned toward where Molly stood in the shadows of the living room. Wearing only those boxers and a cami, her hair mussed as if she'd just crawled out of bed. If only she had just crawled from his bed instead of Uncle Harold's…

"Good thing I brought you more clothes," Mrs. McClintock said as she swung a suitcase toward her daughter. "You don't seem to have brought much with you."

"Books," Eric grunted as he closed his front door and

crossed the living room to his bedroom doorway. "She brought books."

Mrs. McClintock laughed. "She's Molly. Of course she brought books."

"She was supposed to be on her honeymoon," he reminded them—and himself. She was supposed to be married to another man, a man whose ring she still wore. Eric had no right to kiss her, to *want* her.

"Well, I'm not," Molly said.

"No, you're not," Eric agreed. "This is hardly some five-star resort in the Bahamas."

"Bermuda," Mrs. McClintock corrected him. "I think that's the honeymoon Josh intended to surprise you with—after you met up with his parents' cruise ship, in the Greek Isles."

"He mentioned his parents' cruise," Molly remarked, "but I didn't know he intended for us to meet up with their ship. And I didn't know about Bermuda."

"He wanted the honeymoon to be a surprise," her mother explained. "Josh Towers seems to be a man full of surprises."

And money. Bermuda and the Greek islands? Of course, he was a surgeon, rich and successful. He could offer Molly so much more than Eric would ever be able to give her. No wonder she had accepted his proposal—Towers could provide the security she'd lost when her father died.

Eric rubbed a hand along his jaw. "I'm going to take a shower. Nice to see you again, Mrs. McClintock."

Molly stared at Eric's broad back as he turned and walked away. A little sigh slipped from between her lips, but she shook her head, dismissing thoughts of what might have been if he hadn't stopped himself last night.

If her ring hadn't scratched his back as she'd run her hands beneath his shirt...

Her mom cleared her throat, drawing Molly's attention. "Now this is the second time I've caught you two barely dressed. You honestly don't expect me to believe that—"

"Nothing happened," Molly finished the thought for her, then repeated it with more conviction. "Nothing happened."

Her mother sighed. "That's too bad. I have always loved that boy, from the first moment his great-uncle brought him home to Cloverville."

Molly finally realized she always had too—and maybe not just as a friend.

Her mother glanced toward his closed bedroom door and shook her head in wonderment. "Who would have ever guessed that little squirt would grow up to become such a sexy young man?"

"Mom!"

"Don't sound so shocked, honey. I'm a woman as well as a mother." The amusement faded from her mother's face, and she looked away.

"I know you are, Mom." A beautiful woman, who was still young and vivacious. Molly narrowed her eyes as a suspicion nagged at her. "Mom, is something going on with you?"

Her mother's slight shoulders lifted in a shrug. Then she turned away, bustling into the kitchen to fiddle with the coffeepot. "You have always needed caffeine to wake up," she murmured as she filled the pot with water. "Your daddy used to let you sip from his cup when you were little. I warned him that it might stunt your growth."

"And Dad would say that he hoped I'd stay a pretty pixie just like you," Molly remembered.

Her mother blinked as if fighting tears. Memories of her

late husband still hurt her this much? Molly had done the right thing when she'd decided not to marry for love.

"I could use some coffee," she said, to ease her mother's discomfort.

"It would be better if I had fresh beans to grind," her mother said, her hand trembling as she dumped ground coffee into the filter. "But Eric probably doesn't have a grinder anyway. Most bachelors don't think about things like that…."

Molly covered her mother's hand with hers, steadying them both. "What's going on, Mom?"

"You haven't been home much since your father died," her mother remarked. "You didn't come home from college as often as Brenna Kelly did."

"It was too hard." And not just because her father was gone, but because Eric had been gone, too.

"I miss you," her mother said. "I don't know if you've made any decisions, but I wish you would stay in Cloverville."

Molly hadn't decided that yet. She'd worked so long and so hard to become a doctor. All those late nights studying, all those endless days of classes. Wasn't she crazy to walk away from a dream—even if it hadn't been hers?

"I don't know what I'm going to do."

"You'll figure it out," her mom assured her.

She sighed, hoping the older woman was right. "I have decided one thing."

That she couldn't stay with Eric any longer. Her attraction to him only added to her confusion. "You didn't have to bring me more clothes. I'm coming home today, as soon as I get dressed and pack."

"Oh, honey, you *can't* come home."

"What? You just said…"

"That you haven't been home much. But I understand why," her mother assured her. "It never really felt much like home after your father died."

Molly bit her lip, and nodded. "It hasn't."

"Sometimes I wish I could have left, too," her mother admitted. "Maybe I should have sold the house after he died."

"You're thinking about selling now?" Was that what was bothering her?

"I've been thinking about a lot of things." Her mother squeezed Molly's hand. "Like you, I guess I needed to do that—to take some time to work things out in my head and in my heart."

"You've been seeing someone," Molly suddenly realized, her stomach plummeting at the thought of her mother with another man—with *any* man other than her father.

Color flooding her face, Mary McClintock nodded. "Yes."

"It's serious?" she asked, grateful her stomach was empty as it lurched again.

Her mother nodded. "He asked me to marry him."

Molly's breath escaped in a gasp. "But…"

"But what? You think I'm betraying your father if I marry again?"

"N-no," Molly stammered, trying to be understanding; trying to be a friend as well as a daughter to her mother. Theirs had always been a close relationship.

"Well, I do." Mary sighed. "I know in my head that I'm not, that your father would want me to be happy again. But in my heart, I feel like I'm cheating on him—on his memory."

Molly pulled her mother into a hug. "Daddy's been gone eight years. You've spent all that time alone."

Mom shook her head, her chin brushing against her daughter's shoulder. "I wasn't alone. I had my children.

Clayton, you, Colleen…" She pulled back, her mouth stretching into a wide smile. "Rory. But you're all grown up."

"Except for Rory."

"He's getting there," Mom defended her baby, just as she always had. That was probably why he was such a spoiled brat.

Molly snorted in derision. "I'll believe it when I see it."

"No, he's straightening up."

"You don't think he's behind the spiked punch bowl at the wedding?"

Her mother stared at her with suspicion. "How do you know about that?" She smiled as the realization dawned. "You were there. You crashed your own wedding…"

Molly shook her head. "Not the wedding. Just the reception, which I hear you turned into a 'welcome home, Abby' party. Clayton must have loved paying for that."

"I think he loves her," Mom said.

"You wish. You want Abby as your daughter."

"She already is, in my heart."

"And you want Lara as your granddaughter."

"She already is, too. Clayton's just scared to take a chance."

He wasn't the only one.

"Your brother needs time to come around," her mom maintained.

"Is that why you don't want me to come home yet?" Molly asked. "You're matchmaking again."

Her mother lifted a brow in question. "Isn't that what you were up to when you left that note for Abby, asking her not to leave until you came back?"

"Abby's my friend. I haven't seen her much since she left Cloverville. I want to spend some time with her."

"If you'd married Josh, you'd be off on your honeymoon now. You wouldn't have seen her then, either. And we've all visited Abby wherever she's been over the years. Admit it," her mother persisted. "You're doing some matchmaking yourself."

Molly's face heated, and she folded at once. "Guilty. I want Abby for a sister and Lara for a niece," she admitted. "Legally as well as emotionally."

"That's not the only matchmaking I suspect you're doing," her mother said as she continued to study her daughter.

"Who, me?" Molly widened her eyes in innocence. "Match make?"

"Yes, you. You've been reading romance novels since you were eleven."

Molly nodded. "True."

"So what are you up to?"

She glanced toward Eric's bedroom.

"I heard him go out the bedroom slider a while ago," her mother said. "I don't think he wanted to intrude on our conversation."

Or he just wanted to get away from Molly. She suspected the latter. "He moves so quietly," she commented. Then her skin heated as she thought of the previous night, of wrestling with him on the sand, and she added, "And quickly."

"Not quick enough," the older woman retorted.

She hadn't seen him last night, when he'd effortlessly pinned Molly to the sand. "Oh, you'd be surprised how fast he can move."

"Mmm, hmm. I'm not buying that nothing happened between the two of you," her mother insisted. "You've always been a lousy liar."

"Nothing *can* happen between us," Molly said. "We're just friends. But I'm afraid that I might wreck that if I keep imposing on him. Eric is used to living by himself, and this house is too small for me to give him the space he needs."

"But you can't come home yet, Mol. Abby will leave, and Clayton's too proud…"

"Too *stubborn*," Molly corrected her mother, thinking that obstinacy must run in the family genes.

"…to go after her." Her mom ignored her. "And what about your other matchmaking? Brenna and Josh?"

She couldn't suppress a smile. Her mother knew her almost as well as Eric did. "He's a great guy."

"He'd have to be, for you to accept his proposal."

Molly's face heated more. "I shouldn't have done that."

"No, you shouldn't have. But you brought him to Cloverville. He and Brenna wouldn't have met without your involvement."

"I could have just set them up on a date," Molly remarked.

"Yes, well, that certainly would have been less complicated."

"But I was being selfish." She had taken advantage of her friendship with Josh, using him to protect herself.

"You were being a coward."

"That, too." Molly sighed. "I thought it would be better to marry a man I didn't love."

"That makes no sense, Molly." Then her mother nodded. "Oh, you didn't want to wind up like me?"

"You lost it there for a while," Molly gently reminded her.

"I did," her mother agreed with a heavy sigh. "Until I remembered what I had—all those wonderful years with your father. I wouldn't have traded a single one of them."

"But the way it ended…"

"Was excruciatingly painful for us both," she admitted. "But it truly is better to have loved and lost…"

"Than to never have loved at all." Molly sighed. "Like me."

"Oh, you've loved, honey. Just not your fiancé."

She glanced down at the ring she still wore. "I need to give this back to him."

"Yes, you do. But not yet. You need to give him and Brenna time to fall in love first."

Molly thought about their dance at the wedding, the way they had carried the sleeping twins to the car as if the four of them were already a family. She'd called the Kellys to check on Josh and the boys. Mama had assured her that they were all doing better than fine. "I don't think they'll need much more time."

"Give them a week."

"Will that be enough time for Clayton and Abby, too?" Molly lifted a brow. "He's stubborn, remember?"

"Yes, he is," his mother finally admitted. "But he isn't the most stubborn of my children. *You* are."

Molly nodded, unable to argue. Her mother and Eric were both right. "I didn't ask for time alone to figure out whether or not I'm going to get married. I already know that I can't marry Josh."

"*Because* you don't love him."

"He's a nice guy. He deserves a woman who does love him." He deserved Brenna. "I'm using this time to figure out something else."

"Whether or not you can become a doctor," her mom finished for her.

"You knew?"

"Yes, I was in the delivery room with Abby," she

reminded Molly. "I saw you pass out. You hit the floor so hard, you put a dent in the linoleum."

Molly winced. That hadn't been her finest moment. At least she'd done a little better in medical school, with cadavers, than she had in Abby's delivery room. "But I've worked so long and so hard I can't just give it all up."

"But you never really wanted it. You were only becoming a doctor because that's what you *thought* your father wanted."

"He did want that," Molly insisted. Her heart clenched as she remembered all the times she had brought him his meds or fluffed his pillow, and he'd called her Dr. Molly.

Mom shook her head. "No. He only wanted you to be happy."

Were Eric and her mother right? Would she not be letting down her father if she didn't go back to medical school? She had time—at least a week—to figure out her life. She concentrated on her mother now.

"Happiness is all he'd want for you, too, Mom. Go ahead, be happy," she urged. "And don't feel guilty about it."

Her mother sighed, then lifted her shoulders a little higher as if a weight had been lifted from her. "I'm glad you're back home. I really have missed you."

"I'm not home," Molly pointed out. "You won't let me come home."

Her mother glanced around the small cabin, then winked at Molly. "You're home. You're just too stubborn to admit it."

ERIC HAD INTENDED to leave, to pack some things and stay with his friend in Grand Rapids. And yet, having overheard bits and pieces of Molly's conversation with her mother, he hadn't been able to leave. Not until he made sure she was all right.

Once her mother's minivan pulled away from the driveway, he stepped through the slider into the kitchen. Molly stood near the counter, her back to him and her shoulders shaking as if she was weeping.

His heart clenched, accepting her pain as if it was his own. "Molly…" He settled his hands on her shoulders to offer support. "Are you okay?"

"My mother's dating."

"I know," he admitted. "Rory told me."

"So you two talk when you're fishing?"

"Yes." Despite all his siblings, Rory really needed someone to talk to. Right now, so did his oldest sister.

"Do you know *who* she's dating?"

"Mr. Schipper."

Molly turned toward him, her eyes streaming tears—of laughter. "Mr. Schipper? One of our old high-school teachers? Can you imagine—Mom and Mr. Schipper?"

He faked a shudder. "No."

"Remember how he always wore those sweaters with the patches on the elbows and smelled like tobacco smoke?" Molly shuddered, probably for real. "He must smoke a pipe. Mom hates smoke."

"I remember how much you loved him." Eric reminded her of her feelings for their old English teacher. "He was your favorite teacher."

"Yes, but he's not my dad."

Eric pulled her into his arms. "No, he's not. He knows that, Molly. He won't try to be."

She sniffled against his shoulder. "I guess we'll find out Wednesday night."

"What? We?"

"We're going to dinner at his place."

"We're?" His pulse quickened. For so many years he had wanted nothing more than to be a *we* with Molly. But he'd resigned himself a while ago to being only an *I*.

"I'm not going alone," she said, her eyes bright with panic.

"What about your brothers and sister?"

"Mom hasn't told them."

Of course, she would have told Molly first. Mrs. McClintock had always been closest to her oldest daughter, probably because they were so much alike. "Well, Rory figured it out on his own. You don't think Colleen and Clayton have, too?"

"I think they're a little busy with their own lives right now. Clayton resisting his attraction to Abby. And hopefully Colleen resisting the questionable charms of the best man."

"Are you okay with this?" he asked, more concerned about her than her siblings. "With your mom dating?"

She expelled a shaky breath that brushed warmly across his throat. "I think it's more serious than dating."

"Oh."

"That's why I need a friend along." She gazed up at him, her dark eyes intense, and asked, "Are we still friends, Eric?"

"We'll always be friends," he insisted. He had accepted long ago that that was all they would ever be. But every once in a while he needed a reminder—like the engagement ring on her finger.

Chapter Ten

"I thought you lost that thing in the Dumpster," Eric said, tweaking the brim of Molly's straw hat as they walked down the sidewalk on Main Street.

She shook her head. "No, it missed the Dumpster and fell on the ground." And she had picked it up after Pop had left them in the alley Saturday night—four long days ago.

Guilt pulled at her. She hated hiding out, but Mom was right. Clayton and Abby—and Brenna and Josh—needed time to fall in love. She glanced up at Eric, walking close beside her, his bare arm brushing hers. She worried that *she* hadn't needed any time to fall in love.

"Well, if anything should have stayed in the Dumpster, it's that hat," he murmured as he held open the door to Carpenter's Hardware Store, his hand splayed against the glass above her head.

Molly ducked under his arm, her gaze immediately going to his bicep and the barbed-wire tattoo stretched taut around the impressive muscle. When they were in high school, she hadn't understood his wanting the barbed wire despite its popularity. Their tattoos were supposed to have meant something to them. Now she knew what his meant. He'd closed himself off, and the barbed wire was his way of keeping everyone out.

Except her. No matter how much he might like to, he hadn't been able to turn his back on their friendship. As they stepped into the store he caught her around the waist, pulling her between shelves.

"Wha—"

He pressed his palm over her mouth and dragged her behind some boxes Mr. Carpenter had left in the paint aisle. Molly peered around the cardboard, catching a glimpse of bare legs and a blond ponytail swinging against a slender back. "Abby…"

Her heart shifted. She missed Abby so much. With Abby moving away and Molly spending so much time in school and studying, she hadn't seen nearly enough of her friend for many years.

The door swung shut as Abby left the store. "That was close," Molly murmured.

"This isn't a good idea," Eric said.

"But we need lightbulbs."

"I could have gotten them myself," he said. "You didn't need to come along."

Despite what she had claimed in her note, Molly really didn't want time alone. For some reason she much preferred spending her time—all her time—with Eric. "But I'm the one who burned out the bulbs," she reminded him.

"I was kidding," he insisted. "You haven't actually been reading that much."

"I have," she admitted. "At night." Since she couldn't sleep, being just a few yards away from Eric's bed, she read instead. From the dark circles beneath his gray eyes, she suspected he hadn't been sleeping a whole lot more than she was.

"I can buy lightbulbs without you," he pointed out. "I've been doing it for years."

He had been doing a lot of stuff without her. He didn't need her—not in the way that she was afraid she needed him. "The hardware store is right on the way to Mr. Schipper's condo."

"And right in the middle of town, where everyone's sure to see you."

"Good thing I have my hat," she said, tweaking the brim herself.

He sighed and stepped out of the aisle.

"That's who I heard," Mr. Carpenter said, his hearing aide screeching as he fiddled with the controls. "I thought someone came in while I was busy with Abby Hamilton."

Because she'd once driven her car—accidentally, of course—through the front of his store, there had never been much love lost between Abby and Mr. Carpenter. Yet the old man's face softened with affection. "Look at that, she's not doing a half-bad job on my windows." He shook his head, looking bemused.

Molly whirled back to the storefront. She thought Abby had gone, but instead the blonde was pushing a sponge up and down the glass, streaking the windows with soap.

"Molly McClintock?" the old man boomed. "Is that you hiding under that hat? For a minute I thought you were Rosie Hild."

"Told you so," Eric murmured.

"You should let Abby know you're here," Mr. Carpenter said, gesturing toward the front window. Fortunately the glass was too streaky for Abby to see them. "She's been worried about you. All your family has been."

Molly shook her head. "Not my mom. She's known where I've been the whole time."

"Your mama is a sharp one. You've always taken after her the most, until…"

Until she'd jilted a groom? "Please don't tell Abby—or anyone else—that you saw me."

The store owner nodded. "Of course I can keep a secret. I'm not a gossip like *some* of the people in this town."

Since Mr. Carpenter hadn't known where Molly was, she doubted Mrs. Hild was the gossip she'd always been called.

"Of course you're not," Molly agreed.

"Have you talked to your guy yet?" he asked, obviously prying for information.

Molly automatically glanced to Eric, whose jaw had grown so tense that a muscle jumped in his cheek. "My guy?"

"That doctor—the one who makes you pretty?"

"What?" Josh had never made her pretty. She had thought he might make her happy, because she wouldn't have had to risk her heart. Then comprehension dawned. "Oh, you mean he's a plastic surgeon."

"Yeah, that one," Mr. Carpenter said, shaking his head as if dumbfounded about why she had always been called the smart McClintock. "You know—your fiancé?" The old man glanced down at her hand, as if checking for the ring.

With a glance of his own at her hand, Eric walked off— the pressure back in his chest that had been there since Molly had announced her engagement to another man. She had called him so casually with the news—as if he wouldn't care or, worse yet, as if he'd actually be happy for her. Then she had asked him to stand up in the wedding party, and he'd believed she really had forgotten all about *that* night so long ago.

Until she'd kissed him. Now he could think of nothing else. He found the lightbulbs and carried a box toward the cash register. Mr. Carpenter, never one to miss a sale, followed him back.

And so did Molly, proclaiming, "He's not my fiancé."

"You're still wearing his ring," Mr. Carpenter pointed out as he rang up Eric's purchase.

Why was she still wearing Towers's ring? Unless she really had deeper feelings for the guy than she was willing to admit? It looked as if she wasn't quite ready yet to let the doctor go.

"I'm going to give it back," she said, her face hidden beneath the hat as she bowed her head.

"You should do that pretty soon," Mr. Carpenter said. Pitching his voice a decibel lower, he added, "If you don't want it, I think he might have need of it for someone else."

The hat brim bobbed as she lifted her head. "Really?"

The shopkeeper dropped his voice to a conspiratorial whisper. "He and Brenna Kelly have been spending a lot of time together."

"They have?" Molly asked.

"Oh, my, don't that beat all?" Mr. Carpenter said, his eyes wide with shock as he handed back Eric's change. He gestured toward the front of the store.

Some streaks had cleared from the window, so they could see clearly. Abby's back was pressed against the glass as Clayton McClintock passionately kissed her— just as Eric had kissed Molly in the sand the other night.

And as he had kissed her every night since. In his dreams.

"THEY NEVER EVEN NOTICED us walking right past them," Molly said with a laugh as she helped her mother set salad bowls on Mr. Schipper's—Wallace's, as he insisted she and Eric call him now—dining-room table.

Despite being a bachelor his whole life the English teacher had a lovely home, roomy, with sturdy furniture and bookshelves filled with many, many books. "Can you imagine, Mom? My uptight brother making out with Abby Hamilton on Main Street?"

"I always knew she'd be good for him," her mother said with a smile of vindication. "Even your father thought so."

Molly's smile faded as sadness tugged at her along with the memories. "Yes, he did. He loved Abby, too."

"Before he died, he gave your brother my old engagement ring. The one he gave me before I had this anniversary ring." Her mom glanced down at the diamond band that symbolized twenty-five years of marriage—twenty-five years of her life. "I think he hoped Clayton would one day give that ring to Abby."

"Hopefully he will."

"With a little more time, he will," their mother insisted, her voice strong with certainty. Then she glanced toward Mr. Schipper—Wallace—who talked with Eric in the living room and that certainty faded from her face, replaced with a guilty flush.

"That's all you need," Molly said gently. "Just a little more time." It would take time for her, as well, to get used to the idea of her mother dating.

"He's been waiting for me for quite a while already," her mother whispered back. "I'm not sure if he's willing to wait much longer."

"If he loves you, he will."

Mom touched her chin, pointing Molly's face toward Eric. "What about him? How much longer are you going to make him wait? He's loved you since the second grade."

Molly sighed. "You, too? Everyone says that, but

they're wrong. He wouldn't have left for the Marines if he loved me."

"I could say that, too," her mother pointed out. "That your father wouldn't have left me either, if he loved me, but we all know better."

"Daddy didn't have a choice. He died." Eric could have died, too. From his scars, it was pretty clear that he almost had.

"Do you think Eric had a choice?" her mother asked, her voice as firm as if she was defending one of her own children. "He was raised by a soldier. Ever since the second grade he wanted to be a soldier, just like his great-uncle."

"Because he thought that was what his uncle wanted for him," Molly said. He really had been a hypocrite when he'd accused her of only wanting to please her father.

Mom shook her head. "I think his uncle was as worried about him enlisting as you were. Eric became a Marine because it was what *he* wanted. He wanted to be a hero."

He had always been hers—even before his growth spurt. Molly shrugged. "People grow up. They change. In second grade I wanted to be a librarian," she remembered.

"That's fitting," Mr. Schipper said as he joined them in the kitchen. Even during summer vacation he dressed like a teacher, in khakis and a button-down shirt. "I remember that as well as being homecoming queen you were class valedictorian. You would make a wonderful librarian, Molly. You're still the best student I ever had."

"Hey," Eric protested as he walked in behind the older man. "What about me? I was in your class, too."

"You spent more time studying Molly than any of your reading assignments, South." Their former teacher teased them with a wide grin. "I still can't understand why you two went to the prom with other people."

Molly's face heated as she remembered the evening, fighting off her date, an overamorous jock she had gone out with that night only. But she hadn't had to fight him long before Eric had intervened, bloodying the guy's nose.

"I got you thrown out of prom," she said to Eric, as she remembered.

Mr. Schipper shook his head. "As chaperone, that was my duty."

"I don't know who was more ticked off over what happened," Eric mused with a grin. "Your date or mine."

"Mine," Molly insisted. "You broke his nose."

"And you also broke Miss Sneible's heart," Mr. Schipper added. "Yes, you two should have gone to prom together. I think your dates would have both been happier."

Mary McClintock patted her boyfriend's arm. "That's what I always thought, too."

Mr. Schipper covered her hand with his, entwining their fingers. "I doubt there's much about which we disagree."

Mary pulled away, her face flushing with color. "Well, shall we eat before everything gets cold?"

"We cooked, so you two clean up," Molly called out, just as she might have called "shotgun" before a road trip.

"That's good. Because I can't stay," her mother said. "Clayton's taking Rory and the team—and Lara, too—out for pizza after the soccer game. But I want to beat them back to the house."

"So Colleen and Rory won't know where you've been," Mr. Schipper commented, sadness dimming his eyes.

It appeared that the mother snuck around like the daughter, Eric realized, hiding her relationship from everyone in town. Not that he and Molly had a relationship. Despite the kisses, they were only friends.

An hour later Eric stood at the sink, elbow deep in water. As he passed the older man a plate to dry, Mr. Schipper sighed and asked, "How have you done it?"

"Done what?" he asked Wallace.

"Waited so long for Molly?"

Eric glanced over his shoulder, but she wasn't in the kitchen or dining area. So he laughed. "I've hardly been waiting for Molly. I left Cloverville the same time she did. I've only been back a couple of years."

Yet only part of him had come back. Another part of him had stayed behind with the comrades he'd lost, and that included the part of him that thought he deserved any happiness.

"You joined the Marines," Mr. Schipper said with obvious awe. "The whole town is so damn proud of you, boy. You're a hero."

"No. I'm no hero." He pulled his hands from the sink and dried them on a towel. "I just did what I had to do— what anyone else would have done."

And it hadn't been nearly enough. Guilt nagged at him. He should have reenlisted. If not for Uncle Harold's deteriorating condition, he would have. But the old man had been there for him, so Eric had to be there for the major now.

"I suspect that's not entirely true," Mr. Schipper said, his expression as stern as when Eric or Abby had tried to sell him an excuse for not doing their homework. "Just like your claim that you didn't wait for Molly."

"I didn't."

"You haven't married anyone else," the older man pointed out.

"So?" Eric shrugged. "I've dated."

"Anyone seriously?"

"It could have been," he lied. "But she dumped me."

"No one wants to be with a man who's hung up on someone else."

Eric, unwilling to admit the fact that his old teacher was probably speaking the truth, stroked a finger over his scar. "No one wants to wake up to this face every morning."

Mr. Schipper snorted dismissively. "The scar's not that bad."

Not the one on the outside.

"The *right* woman wouldn't even see it," the older man, obviously a romantic as well as an English teacher, maintained.

"Then, I guess I'll know it when I meet her," Eric said with a smile.

"You knew it in the second grade."

"I wasn't in any of your classes until high school. How do you know that old story?"

"I've always been close to the McClintocks. I went to school with Ron and Mary." His eyes dimmed with sadness and a trace of resentment. "I actually dated her before Ron stole her away from me. I think I wasn't much more than seven when I fell for her the first time."

The guy was in deep. Eric couldn't help but pity him. "When you grow up, you outgrow your old crushes."

Mr. Schipper, wearing a pitying expression, shook his head. "No, you don't, son. Not when it's true love."

Chapter Eleven

"He really loves you," Molly told her mother over the phone as she moved a feather duster over every surface in Uncle Harold's bedroom. Eric had gone to visit his uncle, and she had run out of books to read. So she'd decided to occupy herself with housekeeping.

No matter how many times she cleaned this room, dust particles continued to dance in the sunlight and coat every flat surface. At least she hadn't had to make the bed. Overhearing Mr. Schipper's conversation with Eric had kept her awake the night before.

Her mother's sigh rattled the phone. "I know he loves me."

Understanding that her support was needed, she swallowed her own feelings of resentment and asked, "Do you love him?"

"Yes."

She sucked in a breath at the quick flash of pain. Her dad had been gone a long time; her mother was hardly betraying him. So why did it feel as if she was?

"You said he asked you to marry him," Molly recalled. "But you turned him down."

"He's asked me more than once," her mother admitted.

"But you haven't said yes?"

"For the same reason you accepted Joshua's proposal, I turned down Wallace."

Molly sighed. "Because you didn't want to marry for love this time."

"Because I'm a coward. I'm afraid of getting hurt again," Mom admitted.

"You're the strongest woman I know," Molly told her with both respect and pride. She doubted she would have been able to recover from the loss her mother had managed to survive.

If Eric hadn't made it back from the Middle East...

She shivered at the horrific thought. At least she didn't have to worry about that now. He was home.

"Even strong women have weak moments," her mother pointed out.

Molly had never felt weaker than when Eric had kissed her. She was helpless to resist her feelings for him. "Can I come home yet?" she asked.

"No. They all need a little more time, honey."

"Then maybe I should stop by the house and pick up some things." Like a chastity belt.

"I brought you another suitcase," her mother reminded her.

Molly glanced over at the case her mother had left just inside the bedroom door. "I forgot about it."

"Oh, no. You'll have to iron the dress, then," her mother fretted.

"What dress did you pack?" Molly didn't actually have that many clothes at home anymore. Most of her things had been in her apartment and were now packed in a storage unit in Grand Rapids.

"Open the suitcase and see."

Balancing the cordless in the crook of her shoulder, Molly picked up the suitcase and set it on the bed. Then she opened it, to confront a profusion of dark pink satin. "My prom dress?"

"Wallace and I really do think alike. We both agree that you should have gone to your prom with Eric. Now here's your chance."

"Mom, it's a little late for the prom."

"It's never too late, sweetheart."

So her mother and Mr. Schipper did think alike. Or he wouldn't have continued to wait for her all these years.

"Under the dress, I packed balloons and streamers. Make your own prom, honey," her mother advised.

Molly shook her head, amazed at the extent of her mother's matchmaking. "Mom…"

"Eric should still have the tux he rented for the wedding."

"He backed out of being in my wedding," Molly reminded her.

"But he picked up the tux. And according to the rental place, he hasn't brought it back yet."

"He must have forgotten."

"He has been distracted, I bet," the older woman allowed with a girlish giggle.

"He's been going stir-crazy stuck inside this little cabin with me."

"I don't think he minds being alone with you."

"Mom, I don't care if you meddle in other people's lives," she admitted. And then she beseeched her mother, "But stop playing matchmaker for *me*."

"I'll stop when you're happy, honey." The love in her voice, wrapped warmly around Molly's heart.

"Mom…" Molly swallowed hard. "I want you to be

happy, too. So would Daddy. Say yes the next time Wallace asks you to marry him."

"If there's a next time…"

"He'll ask again." A man didn't give up on true love— at least not Mr. Schipper.

Had Eric truly outgrown his crush on her? Molly stroked her fingers over the satin dress. Re-creating their prom with the right dates this time… It was a crazy idea.

"SHE'S NOT HERE."

Paper rustled as Eric tightened his grip on the bag of pastries from Kelly Confections. "Really? Brenna Kelly is not in her office?"

"She hasn't been here much since the wedding," the clerk at the counter commented as she handed back his change. The young girl's face flushed. "Well, the wedding-that-wasn't."

Mr. Kelly, coming out of the kitchen with a tray of fresh doughnuts, laughed as he caught the girl's remark. "Wedding-that-wasn't. It's gonna be Cloverville legend, just like someone driving over Colonel Clover."

Someone. The old man didn't miss much. He obviously knew it wasn't Abby who'd driven over the colonel. He probably knew, like everyone else did, that it had been Colleen.

"So Brenna's really not here?" Eric asked her dad. His sanity and his self-control fraying, he'd needed a friend— any friend other than Molly McClintock—to talk to.

The old man came around the counter, joining Eric in the small dining area, which was crowded with pub tables and coffee-drinking, doughnut-eating customers. "She's helping out Josh at the Manning house."

"The Manning house?"

"Yeah, he bought it for Molly," Pop explained. "As a wedding present."

Trips to Bermuda and the Greek Isles *and* a house? A normal man couldn't compete with a supergroom. "Generous guy," Eric commented, choking down his jealousy.

"Yeah, he's a great guy. And a real romantic," Pop said. "He was going to surprise her when they got back from their honeymoon. Well, you know what actually happened. Josh was the one who wound up getting surprised."

His throat raw, Eric could only nod.

Pop pitched his voice low so none of the coffee crowd overheard him, as he leaned close and whispered, "And Molly wound up spending her honeymoon with you."

"And Towers spent his with Brenna," he replied. Maybe he hadn't just imagined the attraction between them.

Pop nodded. "Well, Josh got possession of the house early, on the condition that he would clear out whatever they left behind. You know the Mannings." Disgusted, he shook his head. "They left him quite a mess."

And so had Molly. A canceled wedding and honeymoon, and a house without a bride to carry over the threshold. Despite his jealousy, he pitied the guy. "So the house needed a lot of work?"

"When he got it, it looked kind of like the inside of that Dumpster Molly fell into the other night." He laughed and then explained, "It needed a serious cleaning and some light remodeling, carpets taken out, hardwood floors stripped and refinished and lots and lots of painting."

"And Brenna's been helping him with that?"

"You know Brenna."

"Take-charge Brenna," Eric said, remembering how the redheaded beauty had mothered them all when they were growing up.

"She's been spending a lot of time with the twins, too," Mr. Kelly added. "She loves those boys of his."

Mimicking Pop by pitching his voice low so no gossips would overhear his question and wait for Mr. Kelly's response, he asked, "What about him?"

"Well, yeah, by working on the house, she's spending time with Josh," Pop replied. "A lot of time."

"No, does she love *him?*" he asked. "Like she loves his sons?"

Mr. Kelly sighed. "She's fighting it, seeing as how Molly's still wearing his ring, but our girl is falling and falling hard."

"Damn it." He should have been relieved, but concern filled Eric instead. Inevitably one of the women he cared about was going to get hurt. Probably Molly. He would have to tell her—if he was truly her friend. He'd have to warn her that if she hid out any longer, she was going to lose her supergroom.

As he walked Eric out the door, Mr. Kelly assured him, "It'll all work out how it's meant to."

"That's what I'm afraid of," Eric admitted. That Molly would wind up marrying the man she'd jilted. Then Brenna, one of his best friends, would be hurt instead.

And Molly would never be his.

"I know you did it," the baker accused him almost idly.

Eric's muscles tensed. "Did what?"

"I know you took her."

He willed a tide of color to keep from flooding his face. "Took who?"

"The bride."

"I don't know what you're talking about," he maintained despite knowing damn well. But he had never made a pact with Mr. Kelly not to lie to him.

"You helped me that morning," Mr. Kelly recalled, "when we loaded the wedding cake into the back of the van. She was on the cake when I rolled it out of the bakery. But when I took the cake out at the hall, she was gone."

"You must be mistaken."

"You stole the bride, boy." Pop slapped his back. "Right off the top of the wedding cake."

"It probably fell off and rolled under one of the seats of the van," he said, dismissing Mr. Kelly's allegations.

The old man laughed—one of his robust, glee-filled chortles. "Next, you're going to be telling me she went out the window."

"Pop—"

"It's okay, boy," Pop assured him. "Like I said, everything's going to work out how it's meant to."

Eric shrugged off his fear and said, "None of this really concerns me."

He had just returned from the VA hospital and feared Corporal Underwood was right. Uncle Harold wouldn't be around much longer, and then neither would Eric. Because once he reenlisted, he would probably be deployed back to the Middle East.

"It concerns you all right," Pop insisted. "I think, as well as stealing that plastic bride, that you just might have stolen the real one, too."

Shaking his head, Eric repeated, "You're mistaken."

About the real one. She had been staying with him nearly a week, and while he'd stolen a few kisses, he certainly hadn't stolen her heart. No, he suspected that belonged to the man whose ring she had yet to remove.

A short truck ride later, his guts knotted with dread, he opened the door to the cabin. He had to tell her that if she didn't do something soon, she was going to lose her groom to her maid of honor.

Music played softly and candles burned on every surface in the living room. He stared up, dumbfounded, at the streamers and balloons. "What the hell?"

Molly stepped out of the bedroom, kicking aside balloons with her high heels, her body encased in a silky pink dress. His heart slammed against his ribs and his body grew hard. She was so damn beautiful. "Wh-what's all this?"

"Welcome to our prom, Eric."

"THIS IS CRAZY," Eric said, kicking aside balloons to shut the front door.

"It's our prom," she repeated, her pulse racing with the fear that he wouldn't play along—and with still more fear that he *would.*

"Our prom was long ago," he reminded her.

"That wasn't *ours,*" she explained. "It wasn't yours and mine. We went with *other* people."

"Until we got kicked out."

She sighed. "You were my hero. My rescuer."

He snorted. "You've never needed rescuing. You'd already kneed the guy." He grimaced as if in commiseration. Yet Eric must not have commiserated much back then, since he'd still fought with the lecherous jock.

"I won't knee you," she promised.

Humor glinted in his gray eyes, and he teased, "Not even if I get fresh?"

Tonight she hoped he would. "Not even."

"I guess I can trust you," he said, "since you haven't kneed me yet."

"Why would I?"

"Oh, are we not talking about the kisses, either?"

"The kisses I initiated?" She shrugged. "What's to talk about?"

He lifted his arms and gestured at the living room. "I'd say we have something to talk about. This is a crazy idea, Molly. We're not in high school anymore."

She smoothed her palms over her satin skirt. "The dress still fits."

"I doubt my tux would."

"Mom says you never brought your tuxedo for the wedding back to the rental place."

He slapped his forehead with the hand not holding the bag from Kelly Confections. "Damn it, I forgot all about that monkey suit."

"So put it on."

"Your mom…" His eyes narrowed. "She brought you that dress the other day. This is *her* idea." He glanced around as if expecting Mary McClintock to jump out with a camera flashing.

Molly glanced around, too, not doubting that her mother might do just that. "She was right, you know. We should have gone together."

"Our dates definitely thought so," he agreed.

"And everyone else in Cloverville."

"When are you going to stop doing what other people expect you to do?" he challenged her.

He had always challenged her. That was why, back in high school, she had thought she could handle nothing more than friendship with him. Then her dad had died and she'd *known* she could handle nothing more than friendship with Eric. Until he had been about to leave her.

"I think I stopped doing what people expect me to do when I went out the window on my wedding day," she reminded him. "I don't think anyone expected *me* to do that."

He laughed in agreement. "I guess you have stopped."

"It took me long enough," she admitted in frustration with herself.

"Better late than never."

"I made a decision." She drew in a deep breath. "I'm not going back to medical school," she said, although guilt tugged at her with the announcement. "I'm *not* going to be a doctor."

He nodded with approval. "So what are you going to be, Molly?"

"Right now, your prom date."

"Molly..."

"Like you said, better late than never. So go put on your tux."

"This is crazy," he murmured again.

"Compared to crashing the wedding reception, this is nothing," she pointed out.

"True," he agreed, rubbing a hand over his face. "At least here no one can see me but you."

Moments later, when he stepped out of his bedroom, she was glad she had him all to herself. The black tux stretched his shoulders wider, made his body seem leaner and even more muscular beneath the pleated shirt and black pants. His face—so distinguished and handsome. 007 had nothing on Eric South.

"The candles were a good idea," he said. "The light's too low for me to scare you."

"You still scare me," she said, her heart beating a crazy rhythm. What she felt for him scared the *hell* out of her, just as it always had. She reached out and stroked her fingers over his cheek, over his scar. "But *this* has never scared me."

His mouth lifted in a half grin. "C'mon. I remember when I first came back. The first time you saw me looking like this, you freaked out."

"Yes, I did," she admitted, closing her eyes as the horror she had felt that day crashed through her again. "All I could think about was how close I had come to losing you."

Despite her emotional admission, Eric's grin widened. "I thought of you when the bomb went off."

Her breath hitched. "You thought of *me* then?"

"I thought… Damn it." He snapped his fingers. "Molly was right."

"That you wouldn't come back?"

His grin faded. "That wasn't an option. I couldn't have you thinking *I told you so* for the rest of eternity."

"You couldn't not come back to *me*," she said. "You'd promised."

He nodded. "And I couldn't break my promise to you."

"I broke my promise to you," she reminded him.

"What promise?"

"The one in second grade—to marry you."

Eric laughed. "I told you before. I can't hold you to a promise you made in second grade."

Can't or don't want to? She didn't have the guts to ask the question that was burning in her mind. But it didn't really matter. She had already decided she didn't want to get married. To anyone. And most especially not Eric. He was the one man with whom she was truly vulnerable.

"Marriage is out," she agreed. "But how about a dance?"

He glanced around, at the balloons and streamers that her mom had provided along with the old dress. "Where's the dance floor?" he asked.

"I was going to move the furniture…"

"But there wasn't any room to put it," he surmised.

"No, we don't need any room," she said. "Remember high school slow dances. Just hold on and sway."

Chapter Twelve

Eric drew in a deep breath and extended his hand to her. When Molly put her hand in his, he rubbed his thumb across her knuckles. "You're not wearing his ring."

"I'm not his." Her throat moved as she swallowed, then gazed into his eyes. "Tonight, I'm yours."

Eric tensed, unable to accept what she claimed. Then he met her stare, and she pulled him into the fathomless depths of her eyes. She tugged her hand free of his. But before he could wonder if she had changed her mind, she lifted both hands to his shoulders, stepped closer and pressed her body against his.

"Molly..."

"Tonight I'm yours, Eric."

Just for tonight she was his. But he had always been hers. Tomorrow would she go back to Towers? He had to share with her what he'd learned at Kelly Confections—that she might be losing her fiancé to Brenna.

"Molly, I need to tell you something...." Before selfishness prevailed and he kept the warning to himself.

"Just dance, Eric."

"There's no room to dance," he reminded her.

Her hand moved from his shoulders to the nape of his neck, her fingers playing with his hair. "Then just hold me."

"I can do that...."

He lifted his hands, sliding them down her back. Then he grasped her hips to pull her closer yet. Her dress rustled as the satin rubbed against his tux, not a breath separating her body from his.

A song streamed out of the speakers, the air vibrating with a low, sexy beat. Eric didn't move his feet—he just held Molly and swayed.

Her soft chocolate-colored curls brushed his chin. Wearing heels, her head barely reached his neck. Her lips brushed his throat as she murmured, "See, this isn't hard."

Every muscle in his body was tense, aching with desire for her, and he could only groan.

Molly shifted, rubbing against his erection. "Oh, I guess something is," she teased with a giggle as girlish as if they were still in high school.

"This is a bad idea," he murmured, confirming something he'd realized the moment he'd opened his door to candlelight and balloons.

Molly's lips brushed his throat again as she asked, "Why is it a bad idea?"

"Because I can't *just* dance with you...."

Molly pulled away until Eric's arms fell back to his sides. Then she caught his hand, linking their fingers, and tugged him toward his bedroom. "Then let's not *just* dance."

"Molly? Are you sure about this?" While she wasn't wearing it, she still must have Towers's ring. She hadn't had a chance to give it back.

In the doorway to his bedroom she paused, then turned

her head—meeting his gaze over her shoulder and the open-book tattoo. "Yes, I'm sure."

He swallowed hard, but he couldn't choke down the words. He had to say them. "But you're still engaged."

"Not tonight, not to Josh."

"But—"

She reached up, pressing her fingers across his lips. "I've never made love with Josh."

Stunned, he pulled her hand away from his mouth and double-checked, "Never?"

"I've only ever made love with you, Eric."

Hope and pride swelled in his chest. He had been her *only* lover? "Molly—"

"I know we're not supposed to talk about that night," she said, "that we both promised to keep it secret. But it happened."

"I didn't talk about it, but I thought about it—so many times throughout the years. Thinking about it kept me alive over there."

"Oh, Eric…"

While he had so many questions for her, right now he didn't want to talk about anything. He wanted to see if the passion between them had been real all those years ago, or if it was just a dream.

Molly's breath caught as Eric dipped his head and kissed her—just a gentle brush of lips against lips. She closed her eyes, tears burning behind her lids at the pure beauty of just a simple kiss.

But she wanted more than kisses—so much more. She lifted her hands between them, sliding them up the pleats of his tuxedo shirt. Muscles rippled beneath her palms. She tugged the shirt free of his pants and undid the studs holding it together. His mouth still pressed to hers, he deepened the kiss, sliding his tongue between her lips.

Molly moaned at the bold invasion. Then finally he touched her. His hands cupped her face, then slid into her hair to tangle the curls she had spent all afternoon taming. But she didn't care; she didn't care about anything but getting closer to Eric.

She pushed his tuxedo jacket and then his shirt from his broad shoulders. He stepped back, pulling his mouth and his hands from her. After undoing the studs in his cuffs, he dropped the garments to the bedroom floor and stood before her, bare to the waist, but for the thin scars that marred the perfection of his muscular chest and broad shoulders.

She expelled a shaky sigh. "You're so damn good looking." Even with the faint marks on his body…

Unwilling—as always—to accept her compliment, he shook his head. Then his gaze moved over her. And light burned within the depths of his gray eyes. "You're the one who's perfect. Just perfect."

"This is perfect," she said. "You and I…"

That was why there had been no one else. No one else had been Eric.

He touched her again, stroking his thumb along the line of her jaw down her throat to where her pulse pounded, frantic with anticipation and excitement. "You're real," he mused as if he'd thought he was dreaming.

She rose on tiptoe, closing the distance between them so that her lips brushed over his. Once. Twice. "I'm real…."

"I have to see…you…all of you." His fingers skimmed her throat, down her bare shoulders—making her skin tingle in the wake of his touch. He reached around her back, fumbling for the zipper tab on her dress.

Molly sucked in a breath, as she'd had to when she raised the zipper herself. And she hadn't been able to clasp the hook. Eight years was a long time. As he dragged down the tab, he skimmed a fingertip along her spine.

She shivered at the sensations racing through her and stepped closer to him. But he moved back.

With the zipper undone, her dress slipped from her body to pool around her feet. She stood before him in only a pair of lace panties.

He groaned. "You're too beautiful to be real."

She smiled in acceptance of his heartfelt compliment. "Eric, touch me again, like you touched me that night...."

His mouth lifted once more in that crooked grin. "That night I was a bumbling kid."

And tonight he was a man—all man. Molly's hands slid down his muscular chest, over his washboard abs to his erection. She winced as she remembered that first time— the pain, the stretching.

"It won't hurt tonight," he promised her.

"It only hurt for a little while," she assured him. Then he had made her feel better. So much better...

He reached for her, but again he touched only her face, his fingers grazing her cheek. And he leaned forward, brushing his mouth across hers. Only their lips touched.

Molly moved closer, stretching her arms around his back, pressing her naked breasts to his chest. He groaned in her mouth and deepened the kiss, thrusting his tongue between her lips. Her legs weakened, and she trembled against him.

Finally his arms closed around her, lifting her. He carried her to the bed and laid her across the chenille spread. "Molly, are you sure?" he asked, his eyes hot as he stared down.

She nodded and arched her back. "Touch me, Eric."

He dropped to his knees, then leaned across her, his lips moving from her shoulder over the slope of her breast before closing around a nipple. With his gentle tug, heat streaked through her body to pool between her legs. She shifted restlessly on the covers.

His left hand moved over her as his lips had—from her shoulder, over her other breast, and his thumb and forefinger closed around that nipple, tugging gently, as he did with his mouth.

She arched her back, biting her lip to hold in a moan of pleasure and frustration. Still it wasn't enough.

His right hand skimmed her side down to her hip. Her stomach clenched as his knuckles brushed across her tummy and he eased his hand inside her panties. His fingers pushed through the curls between her legs, and then found their way inside her.

While his fingers moved in and out, his thumb pressed against her. And his tongue teased her nipple. Tension built inside her, increasing the pressure until it exploded in a flash of heat and sweet release.

She turned her head, tears streaking from her eyes to fall on his pillow. "Eric…"

"I have to have you now," he said, his voice so hoarse she barely recognized it despite having known him for nearly twenty years.

He stood up, his hand shaking as he unclasped his pants and lowered the zipper. He pushed down his pants and briefs and stood naked before her, his long, hard erection straining toward her. He paused only to pull open the nightstand drawer and grab protection. Then he joined her on the bed, his body covering hers—skin, hot and sensitive, rubbing against skin.

"I can't wait," he said as he tore the lace at her hip and pulled off her panties.

Molly couldn't wait, either. She spread her legs and lifted them to wrap tight around his hips. He moved, his erection nudging against her. His gaze intense, he stared into her eyes as he joined them.

Molly bit her lip. It had been so long. But she stretched, then shifted her hips and took him deeper.

He leaned over, brushing his mouth, his tongue, across the lip she'd bitten. "Molly…"

She clutched his shoulders, her nails digging into taut muscle as he moved, with gentle thrusts, in and out of her. She slid her hands from his shoulders down his back, lower, pulling him closer as she arched and lifted, wanting more of the pleasure he'd given her.

The pressure built again, her body taut and hungry, wanting more. She moaned and shifted, moving beneath him, moving with him until her body tensed, exploding with an orgasm even more powerful than the first. "Eric!"

He moved faster, thrusting harder, pulling her closer until his body stilled and he shouted his release. "Oh, my…" he said, shuddering as he collapsed onto the bed beside her. "Oh, Molly…"

She snuggled against his side, his chest heaving as he panted for breath. "We're going to do that again," she warned him. And she wouldn't wait another eight years to admit what she had known for so long. She loved him.

ERIC AWAKENED but kept his eyes closed as he listened for the noise that had brought him out of a deep sleep. But nothing louder than the chirp of birds outside his window drew his attention. So he opened his eyes—to her face.

Molly lay next to him, propped on her elbow, her gaze skimming over him like a caress. "Good morning."

"Good morning." So it hadn't been a dream, last night, the prom, the…

The sheet slipped from her shoulder, baring the sweet, generous curves of breasts, as the cotton fell to her waist. "It's a hell of a good morning," he murmured, reaching for her.

Molly settled against his chest with a sigh, then arched as Eric ran his hands up and down her back. Her breasts pushed against him, the nipples hard points begging for his attention. First he kissed her throat, then her shoulders. After that, he rolled them, so she was on the bottom and he on top, leaning over her. As his lips closed around her nipple, her breath shuddered out. "Eric…"

His body throbbed, demanding that he take her quickly—not like last night, when he had spent hours loving her. He reached into the nightstand, but Molly pulled the foil packet from his hand and tore it open herself.

She pushed against his shoulders, shoving him onto his back. Her soft hair brushed his chest as she leaned over him, sheathing him. Straddling his hips, she rose up to take his erection deep inside her. Clutching his shoulders, she moved—back and forth, up and down, her disjointed rhythm driving him out of his mind.

A groan tore from his throat as he fought the building tension inside his body, trying to wait until she came. He cupped her full breasts, stroking his thumbs back and forth over her hardened nipples. She arched her back, tensed and shuddered, her body trembling as her orgasm poured over him. He rose, driving in and out of her heat until he joined her in oblivion, shouting her name.

Molly dropped onto his chest, her head against his madly

pounding heart. A while later, after they'd caught their breath, her fingers stroked his cheek, gently caressing his scar. "I can't believe some woman dumped you over this...."

Not wanting and not deserving her pity, he tensed. "So you heard that?"

"Yeah, Mr. Schipper... Wallace," she corrected herself, "spoke the truth. She wasn't the right woman."

"No, she wasn't," he agreed. He held the right woman in his arms. But he would eventually have to let her go. Again.

"She was a fool, to not be able to see beyond a scar." She pressed her lips against his cheek. "Especially since it would be so easy to repair—"

Eric rolled her off him, anger adding to his tension. He should have known she'd want to "fix" him. He jerked back the tangled sheets and headed to the bathroom, but she followed him, leaning against the jamb of the open door. His gaze met hers in the mirror. "Molly..."

"Josh is a plastic surgeon, you know."

"Yes, I know, he's one of the doctors who 'makes folks pretty.'" He sarcastically quoted Mr. Carpenter.

She laughed at his bad impersonation. "He's more than that. He's brilliant, really. The best in his field."

Eric was at the hospital so much that he knew Towers's reputation—and he knew that it was well earned. He ignored her as he finished in the bathroom and passed her in the doorway, skin brushing skin. His body tensed in reaction, unable and unwilling to ignore her.

"He doesn't do many elective procedures," Molly explained as she followed Eric back to the bed they'd shared. "He helps burn and accident victims..."

"This was no accident," Eric said, rubbing his knuckles

over his scar. "The explosion was intentional. It was meant to kill me."

"But it didn't. You shouldn't have to carry the scars with you the rest of your life."

"But I'm going to—whether I get my face fixed or not," he pointed out.

"Tell me about that day," she urged him. "Talk about it, Eric. You can tell me anything, you know."

He couldn't tell her about that day. He couldn't tell her about many of his days in the Middle East, not without giving her nightmares. It was bad enough that he had them—except for last night. With her in his bed, in his arms, he had slept peacefully for the first time in a long time.

"Tell me," she beseeched him.

He sighed. "I'll tell you what I should have told you yesterday. You're losing your fiancé."

"He's not my fiancé. I'm not wearing his ring anymore," she reminded him, flashing her naked hand.

"But you still have it." Eric sighed. "Word around town is that he might need it for someone else."

Her eyes brightened. "Who?"

"Brenna." He studied her face, searching for signs of jealousy or regret. "I heard they've been spending a lot of time together."

"That's great," she enthused, her voice ringing with sincerity.

He shook his head. "I don't understand you, Molly. You're still engaged to this guy, but you want him to fall for someone else?"

"We *were* engaged," she corrected him. "And I do want someone to fall in love with him. He's a great guy. He deserves someone who loves him."

"And you don't love him?"

She patted the tangled sheets. "Obviously not."

"Then why did you accept his proposal?" He nodded as realization dawned—along with disappointment and anger. "Oh my God, I get it. You were looking for a way out of medical school. You dropped out when you got engaged. You would have used Josh and his sons as an excuse to not go back."

She sucked in a breath. "I was being selfish, but not that selfish."

"You can swear you didn't even subconsciously use him and his sons?"

She lifted her bare shoulders in a slight shrug. "Maybe. Maybe I did."

"Is that what this is?" he asked, gesturing as she had toward the mussed bed—to the two of them naked. "Another excuse for you to drop out?"

"Eric!"

"Are you using me, too, Molly?"

"You're talking crazy. I've already dropped out. And I've already decided not to go back. I don't need an excuse for anything," she said. Her voice uncharacteristically sharp with anger, she challenged him, "But apparently you do."

"What?" he asked, furrowing his brow in confusion.

"You need an excuse to pull back. You use the scar with other women, but it doesn't bother me," she explained. "So you're turning this around—you're blaming me."

"Less than a week ago you were about to marry another man," Eric pointed out. "You still have his ring, but you're sleeping with me…."

"We actually did very little sleeping," she said.

He swallowed a groan, refusing to let his mind go there,

back to all the things they'd done—all the things he still wanted to do with her. "This isn't about me and what I want."

Because he knew. He'd known since he was seven.

"I think you need more time, Molly, to figure out what you really want. You're jumping from one relationship to another." He left her sitting alone on the bed as he headed back to the bathroom.

"Jumping is better than running. You're running away again—just like you did eight years ago." She snorted in derision. "I guess I should be used to you taking off on me after we make love."

"Molly—"

"Don't worry. You don't have to keep running. I'm moving out, and I'll leave you alone. Just like you want me to."

Chapter Thirteen

Words blurred into ink blotches before Molly's eyes, tears rendering her unable to take refuge where she always had—in books. After leaving Eric's house, she hadn't wanted to go home; she hadn't been ready to face anyone. So she had come here instead, to the library.

And she'd had it to herself for a while. But now she heard the clank of the door and the scrape of shoes against the short pile of the commercial carpeting. So she dashed away her tears with the backs of her hands. Then she picked up the unread book and slipped between the shelves in order to return it—and hide. After a week, she would have to work to break this new habit.

Through the books, she spied on the intruder as she remained on the other side of the shelf that separated the reading area from the stacks. Her lips curved into a smile as she recognized the dark hair and slender build of her younger sister. Colleen had always been a tagalong, forever following around Molly and her friends. God, Molly had missed her. Even though she came home for visits and stayed in the room she had always shared with Colleen, she still didn't see enough of the woman who had been first her sister, then one of her best friends. Silently, she crept around the shelves and stepped closer to Colleen.

"Stupid, stupid," the younger woman murmured as she pressed the heel of her palm against her forehead.

"Hey, don't talk about my sister that way," she admonished her in a whisper.

Colleen whipped around and shouted, "Molly!"

"Shh…" Molly said, glancing toward the front of the library and the elderly librarian who slumped behind the checkout desk, snoring.

Colleen pushed her chair back from the table and launched herself at Molly. Molly's arms closed around her younger sister, her head just reaching Colleen's shoulders. The girl could have been a supermodel, she was that gorgeous. Instead she worked for their brother at the insurance agency he'd taken over when their father died.

"Thank God, you're home!" Colleen said, expelling a breath of relief.

"Yes, I'm home," she confirmed, glancing around the library with satisfaction. Molly had spent so much time here growing up that the library truly felt like home, more like home, in some ways, than the house where their father had died. Since she had decided not to return to medical school, maybe Molly needed to go back to second grade and the career she'd chosen then.

Colleen's dark eyes narrowed. "So, did you leave town? We all thought you were with Eric."

"I don't want to talk about Eric," Molly said.

"Is he okay?" her sister asked, her voice full of concern.

Molly sighed. She didn't want to *think* about him, either. "Yes. Poor Colleen," she teased, "you always had a crush on him."

"Poor Eric," her sister sympathized. "He always had a crush on *you*."

"Not anymore," she murmured.

"What's going on, Molly?" Colleen asked. She must have come straight from the office, as she wore her work uniform of blouse and skirt.

Molly wore jean shorts and a cami. In a hurry to get away before Eric was finished with his shower, she had left most of her stuff at his cabin. She would have to ask someone to retrieve her things later. From the dark circles rimming Colleen's eyes, she didn't dare ask her sister for assistance. She wanted to offer her help instead.

"Are you okay?" Colleen asked.

Molly nodded. "Yes. I'm fine." She was more worried about Colleen right now. "I'm really sorry…"

"No, you don't need to apologize," Colleen said, reminding Molly of Eric. "You've been under so much pressure for years, with college and medical school. Sometimes you just need to take off."

When their father had gotten sick, Colleen had often taken off, probably just needing to get away from that house, from that pain. Molly had understood, and she'd let her sister be. The younger girl had only ever stayed away a few hours before she'd come back home and slipped into bed in the room she'd shared with Molly. Too many nights they'd cried themselves to sleep in that house. She didn't blame Colleen for needing to leave it occasionally.

"So your time alone—it worked?" Colleen asked. "You figured out what you want?"

Molly nodded again. "I figured it out." She swallowed a sigh as she thought of the things Eric had accused her of—using Josh, using *him*. "But that doesn't mean I'll get it."

"So what do you want?" her sister asked.

"Can we talk about it later?" she asked as she settled onto the edge of the table near the pile of books that Colleen had arranged. She picked up one of them and glanced at the title. "You're picking out books to read to the kids at the hospital?"

Colleen nodded, then bit her lip.

"Good choices," Molly approved. She would like to think she'd had something to do with Colleen's love of books. The minute she'd learned to read, she had started reading to her younger siblings. But she couldn't focus on the titles, not with Eric's accusation echoing in her head. "So you've seen Josh?"

"Not at the hospital," Colleen said. "Josh is still on…"

"Our honeymoon?" Except he'd spent it with Brenna, just as she'd spent it with Eric.

Colleen shook her head. "He didn't go anywhere. He stayed in Cloverville, him and Buzz and T.J."

"Where has he stayed?" Molly asked, hoping her sister would confirm that her plan for Josh and Brenna to fall in love had proved successful. "Our house?" she asked, even though she knew better, thanks to her mom's spying.

"With the Kellys," Colleen said. "But just until he gets the Manning house livable for him and the boys."

"He bought the Manning house?" Her mom hadn't told her that. Had Eric also known?

"Josh is moving here," Colleen said. Her throat moved as she swallowed, as if she was choking on emotion, and she continued, "He and Nick Jameson are opening their office. It'll be done soon."

From the way her sister's voice trembled just saying his name, Molly knew Colleen had fallen for Nick—whom she probably wouldn't have gotten involved with if not for Molly's wedding. "I've made such a mess of things."

Colleen laughed.

"Hey, it's not funny!" Molly protested as she held in a laugh of her own, fearing she'd slip into hysteria if she started.

Colleen raised her palms in a placating gesture. "I'm sorry. It's just that I'm used to you being perfect and me being the screwup."

"*I've* never been the perfect one," Molly insisted. "There's only been one perfect McClintock."

"Clayton?"

Molly shook her head. "No, he can be a real pain in the ass. Especially for Abby." Hopefully, he had realized he couldn't live without her and had given her Mom's old engagement ring by now.

"And the perfect McClintock is certainly not Rory," Molly continued. "The little hellion." Eric must have had something big hanging over the teenager's head, because he still hadn't come back to the cabin demanding payment from Molly in exchange for his silence.

Colleen defended their younger brother. "He's actually started to straighten up."

Maybe that was why he hadn't been around. If it was true, she suspected Eric and those fishing *appointments* had helped straighten out the teenage troublemaker. She replayed their conversation. "I was talking about *you*, Colleen. You've always been the perfect one."

"I'm a long way from perfect, Mol. There's something you don't know—"

"I know about you and the colonel," Molly interrupted. Like that night with Eric, she had kept this secret, too. Because she hadn't wanted to add to her younger sister's guilt or pain.

"Abby told you?"

She shook her head. "No, Abby would take a friend's secret to her grave. *You* told us. You were so miserable and guilty when she took off." She squeezed Colleen's shoulder. "She was going to leave anyway. She'd always planned on taking off, but we couldn't convince you of that."

"So you *all* knew my secret?" she asked.

"That secret," Molly said, hoping Colleen realized now that it hadn't mattered. "Tell me your new secret."

"I don't know what you're talking about," Colleen said, but she couldn't meet Molly's gaze.

"Tell me what has you sitting alone in the library, trying not to cry," she demanded, slipping into big-sister mode.

Although Colleen smiled, her eyes were bright. "I'm not crying."

Molly arched a brow.

"Really," Colleen insisted.

"What's his name?" she asked, although she was afraid she already knew it.

After a deep breath, the younger woman spilled. "Nick."

This time Colleen had uttered his name with even more emotion. This wasn't one of her younger sister's crushes— she actually loved him. "Oh, no. It's worse than I thought."

"Certainly hopeless," Colleen said, her eyes dark with misery.

"Then you know," Molly asked, "how he feels about marriage?"

Colleen glanced at the sleeping librarian, then heavily admitted, "Yes."

"But you still fell for him," Molly concluded.

"Like I told you, I'm a long way from perfect."

"No, you're human, Colleen. And we can't help who we

fall in love with." Molly slid off the table to settle wearily into one of the wing chairs, which was upholstered in a book-patterned fabric. "I realize that now."

And she also realized that she'd loved Eric for a long time. If only he loved her—or wasn't afraid to admit he loved her.

"You know, I seriously think he could love me, too," Colleen insisted, her chin lifting with pride and determination. "He just has to let himself."

With frustration Molly commiserated. "Men can be so damn stubborn."

Colleen nodded in agreement. "I know."

Molly reached out and squeezed her sister's hand in sympathy. "I'm so sorry, honey, that you're hurting."

"It's okay." She lifted her chin even higher. "I'm strong enough to handle a broken heart."

Molly smiled with pride in her younger sister. "You are strong—far stronger than I ever realized."

"You're not the only one," Colleen said with a smile. "It's news to me, too."

"Losing Dad was so hard on us, I think we've all been lost for a while." Molly suspected she had lost herself for the longest time.

Because of a few comments her father had made about her becoming a doctor, she had abandoned her dreams— for something he probably hadn't even wanted for her. She'd promised her father she would become a doctor, that she'd make sure no one died of this dreaded disease. He'd patted her head, as if he'd approved of and appreciated her vow. But as Eric had said, her father had only wanted her happiness. Why didn't Eric want that for her? He was supposed to be her friend.

"So you're not going to tell me what happened between

you and Eric?" her younger sister persisted, reminding Molly of earlier days when she had tagged along—quietly—to eavesdrop.

"There's nothing to tell."

Colleen snorted. "There's something. You're just not willing to share it."

No, that was Eric, unwilling to share his life with anyone—not even Molly.

ERIC STEPPED BACK as Brenna Kelly barreled through the front door. His heart rate slowed as the faint hope he'd had that Molly had returned dissipated.

"I know we're supposed to give her space," Brenna said, "but I have to talk to her. Now!"

"She's not here," he said as he closed the front door behind the impatient redhead.

He didn't follow her as she ran to each room of the small cabin, searching for Molly. When she walked back into the living room, Eric leaned against the door and crossed his arms over his chest.

"She's gone," Brenna stated the obvious.

"Yeah." And despite the stuff she'd left behind, he doubted she was coming back.

"Do you have anything to drink?" she asked.

He straightened and headed toward the kitchen, Brenna on his heels. She settled onto one of the stools in front of the lacquered wooden counter.

"Iced tea? Lemonade?" Eric asked, reaching for the handle of the fridge.

"I was thinking of something a little stronger," she said with a heavy sigh.

"I don't have any spiked punch," he warned her.

"Spiked punch?" She narrowed her eyes. "Were you at the wedding?"

"There was no wedding," he reminded her.

"Nope, because *your* friend skipped out before the ceremony. Why did she do that?" Brenna asked.

"*Your* friend," Eric said, "got cold feet." About using Josh and his boys? She wouldn't have done that intentionally. He had been hateful to accuse her of that.

"She's gone. Does that mean her feet warmed up?" Brenna asked as she glanced out the windows at the sun setting over the lake.

His shoulders tense, Eric shrugged. "I don't know what she's going to do."

"Do you think she might want him back?"

"The *GQ* doc?" Instead of opening the fridge, Eric reached into the cupboard above it and extracted a dust-coated bottle of whiskey. He wouldn't blame Molly for going back to Towers. Josh was a nice guy, and *he* was not.

"*GQ* doc?" she repeated. "Is that what he's called around the hospital?"

He nodded.

"So do you think she wants him back?"

He nodded again as jealousy gripped his gut. "Why wouldn't she? He's got the looks. The money."

"The house," she interjected.

"Yeah, I heard he bought the Manning place," Eric admitted.

"You heard right." She stared him down now. "I haven't seen you around at all this past week, yet you know everything that's been going on."

He grinned at her. "I'm a Marine."

"You were a medic, not a spy," she reminded him.

He might have made a better spy than a medic—he hadn't saved nearly enough soldiers. He had to go back. Molly was right—he had pushed her away that morning so that she would leave him before he had to leave her. Again.

His hand tightened around the whiskey bottle. "So the Manning place… It's not the minimansion he probably has in East Grand Rapids, but it's a pretty big house. What? Four, five bedrooms?" Eric remarked as he unscrewed the cap.

"Yeah." Brenna sighed. "He must want more kids—a bigger family."

"Molly would make a great mother." His hands shaking slightly, Eric grabbed two glasses from a cupboard and splashed some whiskey into them. Then he pushed one across the counter to Brenna and lifted the other to his lips.

"Do you think she loves him?"

He nearly choked on the sip he'd taken, the liquid burning his throat. And shrugged. "I don't know what to think."

Brenna tapped her glass against his. "Cheers to that." She downed the fiery liquid in one gulp.

"You're staying here, you know," Eric said as he took another tentative sip from his glass. The whiskey had belonged to Uncle Harold. Eric hadn't opened the bottle since the old man had gone into the VA home. He wasn't much of a drinker.

But Brenna helped herself to another glass, gesturing at him with the bottle as her gaze skimmed him from head to toe. "Why did you and I never…" Before he could answer, she nodded in response to her own question. "Molly."

Molly, for too many years his life—his dreams—had revolved around her. He gripped his drink so tightly the glass shifted beneath his palm, as if about to break. With a sigh, he set the shot glass on the counter and relaxed his fingers, letting it go.

As he had to let her go.

Finally. He'd held on to his crush twenty years too long.

Chapter Fourteen

Molly's hands tightly gripped the wheel as she steered her car down Eric's rutted driveway toward the cabin. Her sister wasn't the only one who had discovered inner strength. Molly had, too. She had the strength to fight for the man she wanted—the man she loved.

But her conviction weakened as she pulled up behind an all-wheel-drive station wagon. Brenna's. With the sun barely streaking the sky with pinks and purples, she had to have spent the night here. Jealousy stung like a cold slap.

Brenna and Eric? They were just friends. But, then, Molly and Josh had been just friends when he'd proposed and she'd accepted. And Eric and Molly... Well, she realized now that they had never been *just* friends.

But Eric and Brenna were both single. They weren't engaged to other people. Maybe they had... Maybe they would...

Her brief spurt of bravery evaporated, and she backed out of the long driveway onto the street and turned her car in the direction of the Kellys'.

Matchmaking schemes notwithstanding, she should have done this a while ago. She owed Josh more than the near-hysterical apology she'd left on his voice mail. In the driveway of the purple, teal and yellow Victorian, she parked her car behind his Suburban.

Reminding herself that she was strong, she walked up the steps of the porch. Glimpsing a shadow behind the gauzy drapes on the windows of the turret-room parlor, she knocked softly on the French doors and held her breath.

The doors jerked open to a dark-haired man who looked more like a movie star than a brilliant surgeon. His voice full of relief, he said, "Thank God you're back."

As he lowered his gaze by the several inches in difference between Brenna's height and Molly's, and met her eyes, the relief turned back into tension. Apparently her matchmaking had been successful, at least halfway. Josh clearly had fallen for Molly's maid of honor.

She smiled at his disappointment. "Somehow I don't think you're talking about me."

"Molly…" Josh closed his eyes and released a breath. "Thank God you're all right."

"Yes." His concern touched her, reminding her why she had accepted his proposal in the first place. He was such a fine person; he didn't deserve to be humiliated as she had undoubtedly humiliated him. "I know you probably hate me."

"No."

"You can't even *look* at me," she said, pointing out that he still hadn't opened his eyes all the way.

A muscle jumped along his jaw as he confessed, "That has nothing to do with what *you* did."

"Josh," she said, amusement creeping into her voice. Being so nice, he obviously felt like a heel about falling for her friend. "You didn't do anything wrong."

He opened his eyes fully, his body tensed as if he braced

himself for an ugly confrontation. "You have no idea what's been going on since you left."

She smiled. "Oh, you'd be surprised what I know."

"I don't want to hurt you," he said, "I know when I proposed I made you a promise."

"When I took off, *I* broke that promise," she interrupted him. "So anything you've done can't hurt me." Only Eric could hurt her—and he had when he'd pushed her away again. Her smile slid away. "So what have you done?"

He dropped his gaze from her as color flooded his face. "I think I'm falling for your best friend."

"Eric?" she teased, even though it was hard to say his name.

"Brenna…"

Satisfaction filled her. Maybe she hadn't screwed up everyone's life—just her own. "Good."

"What?" He pushed a hand through his hair. "You wanted me to fall for someone else?"

She shook her head. "Just Brenna. I realized a while ago that you two were perfect for each other, and I should have broken our engagement then. But I was being selfish."

Maybe Eric was right; maybe she had used Josh and his sons as a way to get out of her deathbed promise to her father. Shame filled her.

"Molly, I'm sorry…"

"I'm the one who should be sorry," she insisted. "I don't love you. I never should have accepted your proposal in the first place."

Josh shook his head. "I don't understand…"

"Neither do I and that's why I took off. I needed to sort out some things." She tapped a fingertip against her temple.

"So, have you?" he asked with friendly concern in spite of everything.

She nodded, then grimaced. "For all the good it's done me. I really made a mess of things."

Josh sighed. "You're not the only one." He pushed a slightly shaking hand through his hair. "I don't even know where Brenna is."

"I think she's with Eric," Molly said sympathetically. "At least I saw her car parked by his cabin."

Josh uttered a short laugh. "So I've lost two women to this man I've never met."

"I think we both know that you never had me. And I never had you. We're just friends, Josh," she said, crossing the room to his side. She took his hand in hers and squeezed it. "That's not enough. We both need—we both *deserve*—more."

"I know."

He deserved Brenna. Hopefully, her friend had fallen for him, too. Then Molly would have no cause for jealousy over Brenna and Eric.

She released his hand, after pressing his engagement ring into his palm. He glanced down at the diamond-and-platinum band, then shoved it into his pocket.

She sighed. "I guess some friends are just friends."

"Is that true of you and Eric South?" he asked, his blue eyes bright as he studied her.

Molly blinked back the tears that were pooling as she realized that the fear she had harbored during high school—the fear that if she and Eric tried to be more than friends she would lose his friendship—had come to pass. "I'm not sure we're even friends anymore."

Josh's arms wrapped around her as he pulled her into a hug, the kind of embrace she might have shared with one of her brothers. "He's a fool, Molly. You're a special woman, and you deserve someone who loves you, too."

"Everyone has told me, for nearly twenty years, that Eric loved me," she told him, laying her head against his chest. "But I always said they were wrong."

"Even though you hoped they were right?"

She nodded. "But I think *I* was right. He doesn't really love me."

And if he didn't love her, she hadn't used him. He'd used her.

"How ARE YOU GOING to manage that box on the back of your moped?" Eric asked as Rory struggled with his oldest sister's books.

The teenager flashed him an impish grin. "So give me the keys to your truck."

"Yeah, right." Eric bit his lip to hold back a grin. "I don't think you even have your permit yet."

Rory shrugged. "Doesn't mean I *can't* drive."

Eric scrutinized the curly-haired kid. "Why do I have a feeling that you might not stop at your house?"

"Molly's back, so that means there's yet another female in my house." He uttered a long-suffering sigh. "I gotta get out of there. Can I stay with you?"

"I don't think your mom would like that." Or Molly. She hadn't sent her brother for her things. Rory, over for their Sunday-afternoon fishing appointment, had volunteered to bring back the stuff she'd left behind. They hadn't been able to go fishing, since Eric's boat was still at the bottom of the lake. Molly had literally turned his life upside down.

"She won't care if I leave," Rory said, his eyes darkening with resentment. "You know what she did, right? She's wearing *his* ring."

"Who?" He'd lost track of their conversation. Was Rory talking about his mother—or Molly? Was Molly wearing Towers's ring again?

"Mom," Rory said, his brow furrowed as if he'd thought either she—or Eric—had gone mad.

Relief eased the pressure on his chest. "Oh."

"She accepted *Wallace's* proposal," Rory said, his resentment even more evident as he uttered his teacher's first name. "She's gonna marry him."

"Tell her congratulations," Eric said. He would tell her himself, but he didn't want to run the risk of seeing Molly again. He saw her enough in his dreams. Naked, her skin flushed with passion as they...

"Right," Rory said with heavy sarcasm.

"I mean it," he said. "Your mom is one brave lady to take another chance on love." To risk again the kind of pain she had already endured.

"But Wallace is a dweeb," Mr. Schipper's future stepson complained.

"Wallace is great," Eric assured him. "You just have to give him a chance."

"I can't believe Mom said yes."

"Like I said, she's brave. She has the guts to take a chance again." Too bad he didn't. But he had decided a while ago that he was better off living his life like Uncle Harold—single.

"I think she'll be happy," Eric predicted. "I think you'll be happy, too, if you let yourself."

Rory shrugged his bony shoulders. "Yeah, maybe it'll be good to have another man around. And Molly might not stick around long."

"Why's that?"

"She'll probably go back to the *GQ* doctor."

Eric winced, regretting that he'd shared that nickname with Rory, and regretting even more that Molly had gone back to her fiancé. "But I thought he and Brenna were…"

Although she was strong, Brenna had to be devastated. He expected she was feeling kind of like he was feeling, with his heart aching for what might have been—if he'd dared to take a chance.

"No." Rory shook his head. "I don't think Brenna wants to be his second choice, you know."

Absolutely. Eric didn't want to be Molly's second choice, her backup plan…

MOLLY LEANED BACK against the porch railing of the Kellys' Victorian house. Relief flooded her because her maid of honor had forgiven her. Brenna seemed to be as in love with Josh as he was with her—even though she was unwilling to admit it.

Molly had already explained her cowardly reason for accepting Josh's proposal, but Brenna, her gaze narrowed on Molly's face, had another question now.

"Why did you change your mind about marrying him?" she asked. "If you're determined to *not* marry someone you love?"

"I changed my mind about that, too." Molly expelled a shaky breath, remembering her "prom night."

"I want the mess."

"Me, too," Brenna admitted.

"Then go after Josh," Molly urged her. "You have my blessing."

"I—I—uh…"

Molly grinned. "You've already gotten involved with him."

Brenna sighed. "I'm sorry I was such a horrible friend. I should have waited to make sure you didn't love him, that you didn't want him back."

Molly pulled her into a quick hug. "Hush. I was the horrible friend, letting you do all the work for the wedding then skipping out. I was so ashamed and so sorry. I called a few times."

"You called?" Brenna asked.

"I talked to Mama and Pop, but they said you were out. And I didn't have the guts to call your cell." Because of her guilt and shame and because it might have messed up her matchmaking scheme. "I didn't know what to say to you, how to apologize."

"Don't worry about it," Brenna assured her friend. "Everything's fine."

Molly shook her head. "It's not fine. You wouldn't be this unhappy if everything was fine."

"It's messy," Brenna admitted.

"I can tell that you already love him," Molly said, holding in a satisfied smile. Brenna would not appreciate her matchmaking. "Does he love you?"

Brenna shook her head, tumbling waves of red hair around her shoulders. "Why would he love me?"

"Because you're perfect for him and Buzz and T.J."

"I'm far from perfect," Brenna said with a shaky laugh. "Or I wouldn't have betrayed our friendship."

"You didn't betray anything," Molly assured her before confessing, "I admit to a little meddling myself. I'd like to see you and Josh together. Happy."

"What about you, Molly? What about your happiness?"

Brenna asked. While she obviously wanted to change the subject away from herself and her feelings, her concern was genuine. "Do you want me to push someone down and sit on him for you?"

"If I thought it would help…" Molly smiled, although she felt like crying. "I guess the old adage is true."

"Which one?"

"Be careful what you wish for," Molly warned. "I didn't want to marry a man I loved. Now I don't have that option."

How could everyone have been so wrong about Eric's feelings for her? Even though she'd spent nearly twenty years denying that he loved her, part of her had believed her friends. Hell, she hadn't just believed—in her heart, she'd known.

She'd felt his love. She wouldn't have come to him that night, wouldn't have given him her innocence, if she hadn't thought he loved her. But still he'd left for the Marines. Because he was scared to love someone and lose her, the way he had lost everyone in his life before his uncle had brought him to Cloverville?

Brenna shook her head, disappointed. "I don't understand your accepting defeat so easily. You've always been the most stubborn one of our group."

"Not as stubborn as Eric," Molly said.

Brenna shook her head. "I've known you a long time, Molly McClintock. And whenever you've set your mind to something you've been single-minded about achieving it."

"I don't want to be a doctor anymore," she admitted.

"You never really did," her friend told her. "But that didn't stop you from working hard, from fighting to get into med school."

She smiled, moved by her friend's defense of her. "This is different…."

"Because you really want this—*him*—you're not going to fight?" Brenna asked. "That makes no sense."

"No, it doesn't," Molly agreed.

"So fight. You never really needed me to sit on your enemies or for Eric to bloody their noses. You might be little, but you're tough."

Molly lifted her chin with pride. "I am tough."

Brenna expelled a breath. "I almost feel sorry for him."

Chapter Fifteen

Hope lifted Eric's spirits as he pulled the truck into the driveway and his headlights glinted off the taillights of another vehicle parked next to his house. Maybe Molly had come back—not to get her things, but to be with him.

But the vehicle was a Suburban, not Molly's small car. And his visitor wasn't petite and feminine. A tall dark-haired guy stood next to his door, in the glow of the mercury lamp that hung on the nearby barn.

"South?" he asked as Eric stepped out of his truck.

He nodded in greeting. "Towers."

"We already met, that night at the American Legion. Call me Josh," the doctor offered his first name, as if they were friends.

Eric didn't care how nice the man was. He was probably going to marry the woman that he—Eric—wanted to have. But he *couldn't* have her. "She's not here."

"Who?" the doctor asked.

"Molly."

"Oh, that's too bad," Josh said. "I thought you and her…"

"No, we're not." Because he'd blown it. He had only himself to blame, but he wanted to blame Towers, too—for already being the kind of man she deserved.

"That's too bad," Josh said again. "The way she talks about you... I can tell she really cares about you."

"We've been friends a long time." But he doubted they were friends anymore. Would she ever forgive him for hurting her twice?

Towers shook his head. "No, she and I are friends. I think you and Molly are something more."

"And that's why you're here?" Eric fisted his hands, ready for a fight. "You want her back?"

"Would you care if I did?" the doctor challenged him.

"Hell, yes!"

"I thought you weren't together like that," the other man teased him, grinning.

"I want her to be happy." He meant that—even though the thought of her being happy with someone else tore up his guts.

"Only you can do something about that."

"What do you mean?"

"She loves *you*."

"Like a friend." Maybe she could have felt more...if Eric had let her.

Towers snorted. "Yeah, right. She loved me like a friend and look how that wound up. She took off on our wedding day."

"That reminds me..." Eric leaned into his truck and popped open the glove compartment. "Here's the bride." He handed the little plastic figurine over to Dr. Josh Towers.

"*You* took her from the top of the cake."

Eric's face heated. "It was stupid, I know. I grabbed it off the cake when I helped Pop load it into the back of the van at the bakery that morning."

"Even before Molly stood me up?" Josh asked, shaking his head. "I guess she was right, that you do know her best."

"You stole her from me, you know," he accused the other man. "She said yes to my proposal first."

"I'm sorry," the doctor said with sincerity. "I didn't know."

"It's okay," Eric assured the other man. "I can hardly hold her to a promise she made in the second grade."

Josh laughed. "Second grade? And I thought *I* rushed into relationships."

Despite the ache in his chest, Eric chuckled, too. "Hey, I might have been young, but I was smart."

"You should ask her again," Josh advised. "To marry you."

"A couple of weeks ago she was going to marry you," he reminded Towers.

"Because she didn't love me." He handed the plastic bride, with her dark hair and white gown, back to Eric. "This is yours. My bride is going to have red hair."

Eric grinned. "You're marrying Brenna?"

"She hasn't said yes yet, but I'm not giving up," he vowed, his blue eyes bright with determination.

"Can you blame her for being hesitant?" Eric asked. "You've only known her a couple of weeks."

"And if I hadn't been engaged to Molly, I think I would have asked her to marry me the first moment we met."

"Guess I'm not the only one who rushes into proposals." He hadn't been in Cloverville long before he had fallen for the little dark-haired girl who'd sat in front of him in Mrs. Miller's class.

"So have you proposed again—since the second grade?" Towers persisted.

Eric shook his head.

"Then take my advice and ask her."

"Why are you here, Towers?" he asked. "To play Dear Abby?"

Josh laughed. "No, I'm here because Molly wanted me to take a look at your scar—to see what I could do for you."

Eric brushed his fingers over the ridge on his left cheek. "She shouldn't have done that." Now he knew he had done the right thing in pushing her away. She didn't love him as he was.

"I told her that I'd already talked to you about it, told you to make an appointment. She wasn't surprised that you hadn't. She said you're using the scar as an excuse to keep people away."

"Maybe Molly doesn't know me as well as I know her." He hadn't needed the scar as an excuse. He'd already grown adept at keeping people away.

"She also says it's because you feel guilty you survived what happened to you."

"And a lot of good soldiers didn't." He sighed. "She does know me."

"And she loves you. She's worried that you've closed yourself off."

He had—actually a long time ago, long before he'd become a Marine. Back when his parents died and then his guardians had given him up. "She should worry about herself—what she's going to do now that she's not going to be a doctor."

"She already has a job."

"Where?"

"At the Cloverville library. She's replaced the retiring librarian."

"She has?" And she hadn't bothered telling him. And she'd sicced her ex-fiancé on him without talking to him herself first. Who was shutting out whom now? He was twenty years too late, but he was finally going to get over his crush on Molly McClintock.

HIS HAND SHAKING slightly, Eric clicked off his cordless phone and set it on the charger. Then he rubbed a hand over his face. It wouldn't be long now…

"Are you all right?" a soft voice asked.

His heart jumped as he turned toward where Molly stood in his living room. She wore a dress, as she had that day she'd dumped them into the lake. The short hem and spaghetti straps left her legs and arms bare.

"I thought you were ignoring me," she said, "but you must not have heard my knock."

"That didn't stop you," he observed, a grin tugging at his mouth despite his mood. Damn, he wasn't quite over Molly McClintock yet—not as his pulse quickened and his breath grew shallow.

"Sorry to disrupt your solitude again," she said. "I know you prefer to be alone."

"What did I say about apologizing?"

She lifted her chin in defiance. "I don't care what you say."

He expelled a ragged sigh. "I wish that was true. Then I wouldn't feel so damn bad about what I said the other morning."

Her dark eyes brightened. "You feel bad?"

"Yeah." He'd been kicking himself ever since.

"You didn't mean it, then?"

"I…"

The brightness dimmed. "You still think I was using you."

"Not on purpose." She was too sweet a person for that.

She shook her head as if disgusted. "And here I thought *I* was the coward."

He'd been called some names over the years but never a coward.

"I agreed to marry Josh because I didn't love him—because I didn't want to wind up like my mom, heartbroken and alone." She sighed. "Because I was a coward. That's the same reason you're pushing me away. Because you're scared."

He couldn't fight the grin this time. "You think I'm scared of you?"

"Oh, I know you're the big, bad Marine," she scoffed, "but when it comes to this—" she gestured between them "—to us, yeah, you're a chicken."

"I'm not scared," he insisted, mentally pulling her barb away from his pride. "I'm cautious."

She snorted.

"I think I have reason to be. Not long ago, you almost married another man," he reminded her.

"I officially gave his ring back a couple of days ago." She smiled. "I think Brenna will be wearing a ring from Josh soon. They love each other."

"Good for them. I'm happy for them." And he was—his heart was hurting a little less than it had been since the morning Molly had left while he was in the shower.

"How about being happy for yourself?" she challenged him.

"What do you mean?"

"Take a chance, Eric. Stop being so cautious."

"Oh, you think I should jump into things like you do? Remember where that got you—crawling out a church window, then winding up in a Dumpster behind the American Legion." He shook his head. "I'd rather be cautious."

"You'd rather be *dead*. Isn't that why you keep your scar?"

"Towers stopped by," he said, a muscle twitching in his cheek as his anger surged back.

"He did?" she asked, her eyes widening with feigned innocence.

"Because you asked him to. You had no right, Molly. Don't try to 'fix' me," he warned her.

Molly sighed. "If only I could. So you turned him down?"

He nodded, then couldn't resist tossing a barb of his own. "Just like you should have when he proposed."

While hurt flashed in her dark eyes, she ignored his comment. "You want to keep the scar because you feel guilty for having lived when some of your fellow Marines died."

"All of them."

Her eyes widened with shock. "Eric?"

"All of them died but me that day." So many good soldiers—good people—and Eric hadn't been able to save any of them. Hell, he'd barely managed to save himself. And if not for his promise to her, to return, he might not have.

"Survivor's guilt," she diagnosed him. "It's not your fault, Eric. I know you tried to save them."

He closed his eyes as guilt and regret washed over him. "I tried. I tried so hard. But I couldn't do anything for them."

"You can do something for them now," she said, her voice softer but closer. She had crossed the distance between them. Her fingers touched his face, his scar.

He blinked his eyes open and met her gaze. He should tell her that he was going back. Soon. The VA hospital had confirmed Corporal Underwood's premonition—more than Uncle Harold's mind was failing. His eighty-five-year-old heart was as well.

"I can do something for them," he agreed. "I can try to save other people."

"You do—as an EMT," she pointed out. "But you can do more. You can do something for yourself."

"What do you mean?"

"You can *live,*" she urged him. She held his gaze, her dark eyes intense and vulnerable. "You can love me."

Molly held her breath, waiting for his response, worrying that he wouldn't admit his feelings and would push her away again. He lifted his hands and closed them around her shoulders, his palms rough against her bare skin.

His gray eyes darkened as he stared down at her. And his fingers tightened their grasp. She closed her eyes, certain he was going to thrust her away from him. But he jerked her forward, crushing her breasts against his chest as he covered her mouth with his.

Nothing tentative or gentle about his kiss, he parted her lips and pushed his tongue inside—all raw desire and desperate need. Molly reached out, grasping his shoulders, to hang on as her world tilted, then righted itself. This was where she belonged—in Eric South's arms.

Breathing hard, he tore his mouth from hers. Then he lifted her, his hands around her thighs, wrapping her legs around his waist as he carried her toward his room. Denim rubbed against her inner thighs. And his erection, hard inside his jeans, pushed against her hips. She wriggled, shifting closer, biting her lip as the pressure of desire built inside her body. Then she leaned forward and bit his neck, her teeth gently nipping skin and muscle.

Eric groaned, and his hands tightened on her thighs. "You're asking for it," he warned her.

"Are you going to give it to me?" she challenged him.

He dropped her, so that she bounced against the mattress. She belonged here, too—in Eric South's bed. As if she were helpless, he undressed her. First he pulled off her sandals, dropping them onto the hardwood floor with a thud. Then he tugged up the hem of her dress, lifting it over her head and letting it fall to the floor, atop her shoes. His hands shaking slightly, he unhooked her bra and slid the straps down her arms until her breasts spilled free.

His breath shuddered out. "You're so damn beautiful."

She arched her back, so that her nipples, puckered and begging for his touch, tilted toward him. "Eric..."

"Oh, I'll get to them," he promised. "I'm going to touch and kiss every single inch of you, Molly McClintock."

Molly shivered in anticipation, knowing that Eric had never broken a promise to her. His hands skimmed down her sides, pushing her panties down her hips. Then he ran his palms down the backs of legs, all the way to her ankles as he pulled off the lace and tossed it over his shoulder.

"You have on too many clothes," she protested his jeans and T-shirt.

"Don't worry about me."

But she did. She had worried about him so long that it had become a habit. Then she'd walked in and found him talking on the phone, looking so serious and sad. She opened her mouth to ask him about it, but his lips covered hers, his tongue sliding into her open mouth, over her tongue, tangling, teasing.

As his hands teased her body. He touched her everywhere but where she wanted, where she needed his touch. His fingers entwined with hers, he lifted her hands above her head. Then he moved his mouth from hers, along her jaw, down her throat. He nipped, his teeth scraping lightly over her skin.

Her pulse pounded as the pressure inside her wound tighter. "Eric, please…"

He untangled their hands but kept her arms above her head as he moved his mouth lower. His soft hair brushed against her skin as he kissed her collarbone then the slope of her breast. Her breath caught as she waited for more—knowing how much pleasure he could give her.

But his lips missed her nipple as he slid his tongue instead along the cleft between her breasts, then farther down, over her rib cage then her navel. He shifted on the mattress, his body sliding to the end of the bed as his head settled between her legs.

His breath feathered against her skin, hot against her inner thighs. Then his mouth closed over her, his tongue slipping inside.

She arched, rising up from the mattress. "Eric!"

"Shh…" he soothed her, his hands moving up her body to close over her breasts. His palms scraped across her nipples as he continued his intimate exploration.

The pressure inside her body built in intensity until tears leaked from her eyes. Then she shuddered as an orgasm slammed through her. "Eric!"

He stood up and tore off his clothes. Then his body, hot and hard and naked, covered hers. He lifted her legs and buried himself inside her.

Molly rose up, kissing his chest, his throat, locking her arms around his neck as he thrust inside her—the pace fast and furious. Another orgasm ripped through her, more powerful than the first. She sobbed at the intensity. Then he joined her, screaming her name as the world shattered around them.

ERIC SPRAWLED across the mattress, his chest heaving as his breathing returned to normal—or as normal as it ever was around Molly.

A soft fingertip traced his satisfied smile. "You look happier now than when I walked in," she observed. "Who was on the phone earlier?"

The tension returned to his body as he replied, "My uncle's doctor."

"Is he all right?" she asked with obvious concern.

He shook his head, his hair rustling against the pillow. "It won't be long now."

"I'm sorry…"

He let her say it this time, and added, "Me, too."

"But he lived a long, full life," she assured him.

"He'd want to go this way, before his mind gets any worse," Eric agreed, trying to find the positives. Molly had taught him that when he'd first moved to Cloverville. And even when her father had gotten sick, she'd stayed positive, trying to find a purpose in what had happened to her dad—to her family. But she'd been wrong—the purpose hadn't been for her to become a doctor, to save people like she hadn't been able to save her father. Her heart was too sensitive to survive such a vocation.

But Eric could save people. "When he's gone, I'm going to re-enlist," he warned her.

Her body stiffened against his side. "You're what?"

"I'm going back."

"But, you, you can't," she stammered. "You were discharged. You got a medical discharge."

"I can be a medic." The limp, the scars, might keep him from active duty, but he could find other ways to help. He had to.

Tears dripped onto his skin, spilling from her big brown eyes. "You can't do this. Not again."

His guts wrenched at the fear and pain on her face. He tried to explain, "I accused you of being selfish, but if I don't go back, I'm being selfish. I owe it to the friends I lost over there—I owe it to them to go back."

"I love you, Eric," she said. "That's why I couldn't marry Josh, why I panicked at the thought of being with any man but you."

"Molly…"

Her voice cracked with a sob, but she cleared her throat and added, "And if you love me, you owe it to me to stay."

His heart shifted, then opened, with her declaration. "I love you, too," he admitted. "I've loved you for so long…."

"But," she said, having heard the word in his voice.

"I can't be who you need me to be," he pointed out.

"And who do I need you to be?" she asked.

"Someone like Towers. Someone with whom you can start a family, build a life. I'm not that guy," he said, hating that he wasn't. "I haven't had a family for so long I don't know how to be part of one. I *can't* be part of one."

"Eric," she said, blinking more tears from her eyes. She ran her fingertips around his bicep, tracing the barbed-wire tattoo. "I always wondered why you'd chosen this. But it was to keep everyone out. You should have added a No Trespassing sign so I would have known not to risk my heart on you."

"Molly…" He hated hurting her; he hadn't meant to.

"You're still a coward," she accused him.

Even though he was going back into war, he silently agreed with her. He was scared of trying to be the man she needed.

FACE WARM with the sunlight streaking through the blinds, Molly opened her eyes. Then she stretched, her arms sliding across the empty space next to her. He was gone.

No note. He'd left her. Just like last time. It didn't matter how much she loved him, how much she wanted him. She had to accept that this was one fight she couldn't win—no matter how stubborn she was.

Eric would never love her as much as she loved him. If he did, he wouldn't be able to leave her again. She turned her face into his pillow and she wept as hard as she had the day her dad died, her heart just as empty and broken.

This was the loss she'd tried to avoid, the reason she'd accepted Josh's proposal instead of going after the man she really loved. Because she had known then, she would only get hurt.

Chapter Sixteen

Could he do it again? Could he really leave her? Eric wondered as he poured himself a much-needed cup of coffee. Yet the pot in the staff lounge had burned low, leaving only sludge. He grimaced as he took a sip, but he needed the caffeine. He hadn't slept at all the night before; he'd watched her sleep instead, watching her lashes flutter against her cheeks as she dreamed.

Of what? Of him? Of the life they might have had if he wasn't a coward. She was right. Despite the medals he'd locked away in a drawer, he was no hero.

A real hero would step up, would be the kind of guy she wanted, she deserved.

"Eric?" a gruff voice called his name.

Drawing in a ragged breath, he turned only fractionally, meeting Nick Jameson's gaze over his shoulder. "Yeah. Hey, Doctor, do you need something?"

"I thought you were off the clock."

He shrugged. He had stopped by the VA hospital that morning, checking on his uncle before his shift started. He'd probably stop by again, before he headed home. Molly would be gone, the last of her things packed up. "I've got no place else to be."

"I hear you," Jameson commiserated, his green eyes dark with his own regrets.

Eric sighed again. "But I've got no one but myself to blame."

"I hear you," Nick repeated.

The doctor's raw honesty surprised Eric, who recognized a man suffering his own heartache. "You know my name—Eric South." He turned fully and extended the hand not holding a coffee mug to Nick.

Dr. Jameson hesitated a moment before taking his outstretched hand, his gaze drawn to Eric's scar. Finally he offered his name, "Nick Jameson."

Eric released his hand, then touched his scar. He was used to people staring at it. With a weak attempt at humor, he said, "You should see the other guy."

The doctor shook his head. "A fist didn't do that damage. I'd say jagged metal, maybe glass fragments. Car accident?"

"It was no accident," Eric told him the same thing he had Molly, but he wouldn't—he couldn't—share much more. "Afghanistan," he added, knowing that was probably explanation enough.

Nick nodded. "How long have you been back?"

"I've been back a couple of years."

The doctor nodded again. "You were a medic over there," he surmised.

"Yes, with the Marine Corps."

"You did a good job with Westin."

"Heard you did, too." While Eric had delivered the accident victim to the E.R., Nick had performed the surgery that had saved the guy's leg.

The doctor shrugged off the comment.

"Couldn't have been easy," Eric remarked, noting the rash on Nick's forearms.

His voice defensive with pride, Nick began, "No…"

"Because of your poison ivy," Eric explained, soothing the arrogant surgeon's obviously wounded pride. "I break out every time I set foot near Cloverville Park."

He remembered the blond-haired guy carrying the picnic basket, then spreading the blanket across the grass. Colleen must not have stayed outside the gate watching him.

Nick glanced down at his rash, which was already dried and healing. "I gave myself a cortisone injection and made sure I wasn't contagious before I came back to work."

Eric nodded. "Still damn uncomfortable. So where'd you get it?"

"Cloverville Park. But you knew that," Nick surmised, his green eyes narrowed.

Eric grinned. "You're the other one of the *GQ* docs."

A muscle jumped in Nick's jaw. He obviously didn't appreciate the nickname.

"You're the best man," Eric continued. "Gossip around town is that you were spending time with Colleen McClintock." Not that he listened to gossip.

Nick sighed. "I should have known someone would hear about us."

"There are no secrets in Cloverville." Except his and Molly's. No one had ever guessed what they'd done before he left for the Marines. No one but them knew they had been each other's first. Him Molly's only. If he left her, she would find someone else—eventually. She wouldn't wait for him again. His chest ached with the realization.

Nick grinned. "No, there aren't. You were supposed to be in the wedding party, too."

Eric nodded. "Yup, but there was no wedding."

"No, there wasn't." Jameson studied him, as if trying to figure him out. "So you're where Molly McClintock was staying."

Eric nodded. "She's gone home now." His house—his bed—his life—would be so empty without her.

"So you're in love with her," Jameson guessed.

"For almost twenty years," he admitted, not bothering to lie to Nick or himself.

"Then how come she almost married my friend and not you?" the surgeon wondered aloud.

"She was engaged to me first," Eric shared.

"So she's done this before, promised to marry a guy and then ran off?" Nick asked, his voice sharp with disapproval.

Eric shook his head in defense of the woman he loved. "I was the one who ran off." He sighed and admitted, "And I was just about to do it again."

"You're leaving? Just Cloverville or the hospital?"

"The country," Eric shared. He understood why Towers had chosen this guy as his best man—he was easy to talk to. Or maybe Eric just needed someone, anyone, to talk to since he'd pushed away his best friend. Molly.

"Now, that's really running…"

"Yeah."

"It would be a damn shame if you left the hospital," Nick said. "I've noticed your work before. You're the best damn EMT we've got."

Eric nodded, accepting the compliment. He was good at his job. "That's why I wanted to go back. Maybe I could do more good this time." Maybe he could save more soldiers.

"You're doing good here," Nick praised him. "You've saved a lot of lives."

"You're the surgeon."

"But you're the one who keeps them alive until I can help them," Nick pointed out. "We need guys like you *here,* too."

As long as he was saving people, did it matter where he did it? Could he keep his job here, could he build the life here that he had been scared to imagine? A life with Molly? His heart thumped against his ribs as he let it fill with hope.

"Somehow I think Molly McClintock needs you, too," Nick suggested. "And I think I finally have the answer to my question."

"What question?"

"Why she stood up a great guy like Josh," he explained. "She was already in love with another man."

"That's what she said," Eric admitted.

"And you didn't believe her?"

"I think I was afraid to believe her."

"This is scary business," Nick agreed with a heavy sigh. "This falling in love…"

And it was about damn time Eric stopped being a coward and running from his feelings and from Molly.

MOLLY BREATHED DEEP, inhaling the dusty aroma of books as if it were an expensive perfume. "I'm home," she declared—with pride. Yet not enough pride to fill the emptiness and longing inside her.

To find her dream, she had gone back to second grade, to the career she'd envisioned for herself then. To find her true love, she had also gone back to second grade—to Eric. But he'd made it painfully clear that he didn't want her love or her.

Her breath caught and then shuddered out in a ragged sigh. If he loved her, he wouldn't leave her. Again.

The front door rattled, then clanked as it opened and slammed shut. Even though no one else was in the library to disturb this near closing time, Molly stepped up to the duties of her job. "Shh…"

Her irritation faded, replaced with pain, as the person stepped into her view. Clad in the white shirt and navy blue pants of his EMT uniform, he must have come directly from work. "Is it your uncle?" she asked. "Is he…"

Eric shook his head. "He's alive." He walked closer until only the checkout desk separated them. "And thanks to you, so am I."

"For now." She closed her eyes to hold in the tears. She'd already wept too many over him.

"Hopefully for a long time," he said.

Her eyes still closed, she shook her head. "It's too dangerous…"

"You don't have to tell me," he agreed.

"No." She opened her eyes, and resignation pulled her shoulders down as if she carried a stack of encyclopedias on her back. "I don't have to tell you because you won't listen to anything I say. You didn't last time, and you won't this time."

"No, I won't," he admitted. But he reached across the desk, brushing his fingertips along her jaw.

"Eric…" Emotion choked her, but she swallowed it down and summoned her pride. "Just leave me alone. Please, just leave me alone."

His gray eyes warm, he shook his head. "I can't…"

"Eric, please," she murmured, her chest aching with a pain so intense she feared it would never go away—even if he did.

"I'm not going to re-enlist. I can't leave you again, Molly."

Did she dare to hope he spoke the truth? Eric had never lied to her before. The pressure on her chest began to ease. "Really? You've changed your mind?"

"I may be a little slow, but I'm not stupid," he joked.

She reached across the desk and smacked his shoulder. "Don't tease me. Not now…"

"I hate that I hurt you," he said, his voice thick with regret. "I'm sorry, so sorry."

She pressed her fingers across his lips. "Quit."

He shook his head, knocking her hand from his mouth. "I can't quit. I tried," he admitted, "but I never got over my crush on you."

Molly ducked around the desk. "Is that all this is? A crush?"

He shook his head again as he closed the distance between them, wrapping his arms around her waist. "It was never just a crush."

She drew in a breath, having to ask the question that had haunted her the past eight years. "Then how did you leave me?"

"I didn't trust that you really loved me," he explained. "We'd known each other since the second grade, and you never once acted like anything more than my friend."

"But that night…"

"You didn't want me to go." He sighed, his eyes dark with regret for having hurt her. "You'd just lost your dad. We were close. You didn't want to lose me, too. You had to have known how I felt about you—how I always felt about you."

"Colleen and Brenna and Abby all insisted that you loved me." Her breath hitched as she relived that night. "But still you were going…"

"So you came to me, you made love to me."

"Didn't that tell you something?" she wondered. "Didn't that prove my love?"

"It proved your friendship," he said. "It proved that you didn't want me to get hurt. But I hurt you instead. And I've spent the past eight years regretting that. But I never regretted what we did. It was right that we were each other's first."

"Because we were each other's first loves," she said. "*Only* love. I wish you would have realized that then. I wish you would have trusted my love."

"But you've always been so generous, Molly, so giving…"

"It was more than that."

"I know that now." He kissed her—just a light brush of lips across lips. Then he murmured against her mouth, "It was true love."

"Still is." But she pulled out of his arms.

His eyes filled with confusion at her reaction as his empty arms fell back to his sides. "Molly?"

She lifted a set of keys from the desk and jangled them in the air. Then she walked over to the front door and locked it. "The library's closed." There had always been something she'd wanted to do in it after dark—something that had nothing to do with reading.

She returned to him and reached for the buttons on his shirt. "As much as I love you in uniform," she said as excitement quickened her pulse, "I'd love you more out of it."

"Molly…"

She rose on tiptoe and pressed her mouth to his—to silence his protest. But Eric wasn't protesting as he reached under her dress and pulled down her panties. They made love fast and furiously, standing up with her legs locked around his waist as he drove deep inside her.

But even when they weren't making love he was deep inside her. He had always been.

His mouth imitated what his body was doing to her, his tongue sliding in and out of her lips. His hands gripped her butt, then slid up her back under her dress—pressing her against the chest she'd bared. The shirt hung from his shoulders, only the zipper of his pants undone.

She tensed, then shuddered as an orgasm rippled through her. Then Eric shouted, joining her in sweet release.

"That was crazy," he murmured as he dropped onto a chair with her in his lap, held close to his madly pounding heart. "I'm sorry it was so fast…."

"We've gone slow before," she said. "We'll do it slow again."

"We'll do it all night—every night."

She grinned at his ambition. But she wouldn't try to stop him from achieving his dream. "Besides, we've already taken too much time."

Time wasted like Mrs. Hild had wasted time she could have spent with her Ernest.

"So it's true," Eric said, gesturing around at the shelves of books. "You're the new librarian."

Molly nodded, bumping her forehead against his throat as she burrowed against his neck—never able to get close enough to him. "I was going to tell you the other day, but…" He'd shared his devastating news first. "I have to take a few more classes and get a degree in library sciences."

"But they still gave you the job?"

"They trust me to take the classes and finish the degree. I hope you trust me now, too, Eric." Running her fingers along his jaw, she tipped his face to hers and held his gaze, as she promised, "I will never leave you like the other people in your life have."

"I know." He not only spoke the words; he meant them. He knew Molly—better than anyone else. "And that's good because I'd hate for you to go out a window on our wedding day."

"Oh, we're going to have a wedding day?" she asked with mock innocence as she blinked her thick lashes.

"Don't act surprised," he said with a grin. "We've been engaged for twenty years. I think it's about time we make it official."

"Yeah, it's about time." She kissed him, her lips silky soft against his. "You know everyone else is getting married, too. Abby and Clayton. He finally gave her my mother's engagement ring."

"Colleen, too. Nick's probably asking her right now," Eric said.

"And Brenna and Josh. She's too smart to keep turning him down."

"And your mom and Wallace," he gently reminded her.

She nodded. "And Wallace and Mom."

"Are you okay with that?"

She smiled. "My dad would want her to be happy. And so do I. And you were right. All he had ever wanted for me was happiness."

"Then I'll do my best to make you happy, Molly McClintock, for the rest of our lives."

HE INTENDED TO REPEAT that vow at their wedding—just a few short days later. Because they had been engaged the longest—nearly twenty years—everyone had agreed that they should get married first. Of course he'd threatened a couple of them with the bloody nose he'd given Molly's first prom date.

"You know I could have fixed it," Josh said as Eric stepped out of the kitchen slider and joined the doctor on the back deck.

Gazing out over the rows of chairs that had been arranged on the lawn between the cabin and the lake, Eric brushed his knuckles across his scar, thinking that was what the doctor referred to. "I couldn't wait."

"I know—you threatened me with a bloody nose," Josh reminded him. "Which was an empty threat since I could have fixed whatever damage you did."

"To our pretty faces," the other *GQ* doctor piped up.

"How 'bout you fix this scar," Eric said, "when Molly and I get back from our honeymoon?"

Josh clasped his shoulder. "I'd love to. Our office is officially open now, so call for an appointment."

"Sunday is supposed to be our appointment," Rory grumbled as he and his brother joined the other groomsmen on the deck. "For fishing."

"Your sister sank my boat," Eric reminded the teenager. "Anyway, I need you for something a little more important than fishing."

A grin spread across Rory's still-boyish face. "Yeah, I'm your best man."

"That remains to be seen, little brother," Clayton cautioned him, but his dark eyes already filled with approval rather than censure.

"You guys gotta stay here and get your women," Rory said as the preacher signaled from the dock.

As Eric walked down the aisle with his best man, several

of the guests reached up and caught his hand, offering comments as well as congratulations: "'Bout time."

"Always knew you two would wind up together."

And Pop's, "See, son, it all worked out how it was meant to."

Eric grinned and slapped the older man on the back. "Yes, it did." He paused again in the first row and knelt beside his great-uncle's wheelchair. "I'm glad you're here."

Recognition filled the old man's gray eyes. "I wouldn't have missed this for anything. I'm so proud of you, boy."

Corporal Underwood, his chair pulled next to Uncle Harold's, winked and nodded.

Eric stepped onto the white-carpeted dock, walking beside his best man. Then he stopped next to the preacher, within hearing distance of shore, and turned back to his and Molly's guests—and wedding party.

Rory turned to him with his impish grin. "So you worried she's gonna go out a window?"

"I know she's going to," Eric said, peering around the couples now that walked arm in arm down the aisle between the chairs. Clayton and Abby. Josh and Brenna. Nick and Colleen.

Finally, he saw her, stepping through his—*their*—bedroom slider onto the deck. She wore the dress with her veil this time. In the white strapless lace-and-satin gown, she looked like an angel, as if she'd stepped right off the top of a cake. Then the bridal march began, Rosie Hild playing the tune on the organ, which sat on a platform on the sand. And all the guests rose and turned toward his bride, hiding her from his view.

"You didn't see Eric before the wedding?" her mom asked as she held Molly's arm to escort her down the aisle.

"It wouldn't matter if I had—or if I'd walked under a ladder and crossed the path of a black cat on my way to see him," Molly assured her. "Nothing is going to stop me from marrying the man I love."

Her mom grinned as they walked past Wallace, who sat with the Kellys. "Me neither."

"Good." When her mother had pulled out her lipstick earlier, Molly had seen the plane tickets to Vegas in the older woman's purse. Departure was scheduled for that evening. Somehow it was appropriate that she and her mother share an anniversary.

"I couldn't be happier today," her mother said, tears sparkling in her brown eyes like sunlight sparkled on the water of the small fishing lake.

"Me neither."

Mary McClintock tightened her grip on Molly's arm— as they stepped together onto the dock—joining the three men already there. Molly didn't see the other two; she saw only her groom, looking dashing in his black tux and crisp white pleated dress shirt. Through the lace of her veil, Molly met Eric's gray gaze and everyone and everything else faded away. She barely heard the preacher's words.

"We're gathered here today for the wedding of this man to this woman…"

"About damn time," someone—probably Pop or Mr. Carpenter—commented from the rows of guests.

Someone else twittered.

"Who gives this woman in marriage?" Reverend Howard asked.

"I do," said Mary McClintock, her voice full of pride. She lifted her daughter's veil and kissed her cheek, then she kissed Eric's, right on his scar. But she didn't join the other guests; she just stepped into her place at Molly's side, as her matron of honor.

Eric reached out, taking Molly's hands in his. He rubbed his thumbs across her bare knuckles. His voice shaking with emotion, he repeated the traditional vows. Then he added his own, "I have already loved you forever, Molly. And I will continue to love you until I draw my last breath…."

Tears blurred the sight of his handsome face. She blinked and returned his promise, "I will love you for eternity, Eric South."

"You are my best friend," he told her. "My heart. My soul."

The tears streaked down her face now. At her side, her mother sniffled, too. And many of the wedding party and the guests dabbed their eyes.

Even Rory blinked hard as he handed over the rings.

The preacher held his hand over the bands, blessing them. "These rings are a symbol of your unbreakable bond."

They didn't need rings to symbolize what they already knew—what they'd known in their hearts since they were seven. But satisfaction, as well as love, filled Molly as Eric slid the wedding band onto her finger.

She was *finally* a bride.

Epilogue

Twenty years later...

Red and white fairy lights and balloons brightened the interior of the Cloverville American Legion post.

"I don't understand what this party is," Molly's teenage daughter, Ronni, said, as the thin brunette settled onto a chair next to her mother.

"It's an anniversary."

"Of what? This isn't the date when you and Dad were married."

"It was supposed to be my wedding day," she admitted with a smile. "To Josh Towers."

"You were supposed to marry T.J. and Jamie's dad?" They'd stopped calling Nicholas James Towers Buzz when his dark hair had grown halfway down his back. But he'd cut it when he and his twin had started medical school a couple of years ago. After their internships and residencies, they planned on joining their father and godfather's private practice in Cloverville. "You were going to marry him instead of Dad?"

"I had accepted his proposal."

Ronni's gray eyes widened in shock and wonder. "But Josh is *hot*, Mom."

Still, twenty years later, he was. And he was also blissfully happy with Brenna—with whom he swayed on the dance floor among all the twirling children. Many of the kids were theirs; some had their mother's glorious red hair, others their father's devastating combination of black hair and blue eyes.

Molly's mother, in the arms of her husband, Wallace, watched all the children, her dark eyes warm with affection, as if they were all her grandchildren. Molly made a mental note to warn the older ones about her mother's matchmaking.

Then her gaze followed her husband, in a dark suit, as he closed the short distance between them. And she figured she'd leave Mom be; she knew what she was doing, after all.

"Your father is hot, too," Molly insisted as he joined them, sliding into the chair next to her so close that his thigh brushed hers. She tingled with awareness, their passion every bit as hot as it has been twenty—and twenty-eight—years ago.

"But, Dad…" Ronni's face colored. "I saw pictures of you before Uncle Josh fixed your scar."

He grinned. "Yes, I had a face only a mother could love."

"And the right woman."

"You're the right woman, wife," he agreed, pressing his mouth to hers in a kiss both deep and beautiful.

"Ewww…" their daughter groaned. "You guys are sick."

"What's sick?" their younger daughter, Rosie, asked, catching only her sister's comment as she left her brother, Harry, on the dance floor.

"That hat is sick," Ronni told her sister.

Eric tweaked the brim of the old straw hat and asked the ten-year-old, "Where'd you find that?"

"In the back of Mom's closet."

"I thought you might have pulled it out of a Dumpster," he teased.

Molly smacked his shoulder. "I'm the one you pulled out of a Dumpster."

"What?" both daughters shrieked, in shock.

"On the same day she'd gone out the church window instead of marrying Joshua Towers," their father added.

"It's like we don't know you at all," Ronni murmured, glancing up as her uncle joined them.

Rory gestured toward the punch Eric had brought them. "Do I need to check to see if that's spiked?" he asked, his voice so deep now and full of authority.

"Nope, Sheriff," Eric assured his brother-in-law. "It's nonalcoholic, just like the label on the punch bowl says." Rory hadn't been back that long from his second tour as a Marine before Cloverville had elected the former trouble-maker sheriff.

As if the thought of former troublemakers had conjured her up, Abby Hamilton-McClintock joined them; her bright blue eyes still alight with mischief.

"Uh-oh," Rory said, shaking his head. "Here's America's most wanted."

"*My* most wanted," Clayton said as he wrapped his arms around his petite blond wife. Ever since Abby had returned to Cloverville twenty years ago, he'd never let her go. "But it's a good thing our oldest just passed the bar."

She would probably have to use her law license to keep her younger brother, Clay Jr., out of trouble. But Abby took it personally and jabbed an elbow into her husband's ribs—gently—and protested, "*I* don't get in trouble anymore."

"You just make it," Clayton teased his wife.

"Lara passed the bar?" Pride filled Molly. "Tell my niece congratulations."

"She just walked in now," Eric noted, still missing nothing. The petite blond looked exactly like her mother had twenty years ago. Gorgeous.

Behind Lara, hand in hand, walked in Colleen and Nick. Her older sister noted the wood chips and grass stuck to Colleen's dress and tangled in her thick, dark hair; she and Nick still spent too much time in the park. She didn't know how they managed, with all the kids they'd raised. Even though Colleen hadn't been able to conceive children, they'd fostered many, many runaways over the past twenty years. Most of them were party guests.

"So what is this?" Ronni asked again, gesturing around at the lights and balloons.

"It's the twenty-year anniversary of the wedding-that-wasn't," explained her uncle Nick.

"A wedding party?" Rosie asked, having only caught a portion of what her uncle had said.

Happiness complete, Molly gazed around at all her family and friends. "No, *this* is my wedding party."

* * * * *

Here's a sneak peek at
THE CEO'S CHRISTMAS PROPOSITION,
the first in USA TODAY *bestselling author*
Merline Lovelace's HOLIDAYS ABROAD *trilogy*
coming in November 2008.

American Devon McShay is about to get the Christmas
surprise of a lifetime when she meets her new client,
sexy billionaire Caleb Logan, for the very first time.

Available November 2008

Her breath whistled out in a sigh of relief when he exited Customs. Devon recognized him right away from the newspaper and magazine articles her friend and partner Sabrina had looked up during her frantic prep work.

Caleb John Logan, Jr. Thirty-one. Six-two. With jet-black hair, laser-blue eyes and a linebacker's shoulders under his charcoal-gray cashmere overcoat. His jaw-dropping good looks didn't score him any points with Devon. She'd learned the hard way not to trust handsome heartbreakers like Cal Logan.

But he was a client. An important one. And she was willing to give someone who'd served a hitch in the marines before earning a B.S. from the University of Oregon, an MBA from Stanford and his first million at the ripe old age of twenty-six the benefit of the doubt.

Right up until he spotted the hot-pink pashmina, that is.

Devon knew the flash of color was more visible than the sign she held up with his name on it. So she wasn't surprised when Logan picked her out of the crowd and cut in her direction. She'd just plastered on her best business-woman smile when he whipped an arm around her waist.

The next moment she was sprawled against his cashmere-covered chest.

"Hello, brown eyes."

Swooping down, he covered her mouth with his.

Sheer astonishment kept Devon rooted to the spot for a few seconds while her mind whirled chaotically. Her first thought was that her client had downed a few too many drinks during the long flight. Her second, that he'd mistaken the kind of escort and consulting services her company provided. Her third shoved everything else out of her head.

The man could kiss!

His mouth moved over hers with a skill that ignited sparks at a half dozen flash points throughout her body. Devon hadn't experienced that kind of spontaneous combustion in a while. A *long* while.

The sparks were still popping when she pushed off his chest, only now they fueled a flush of anger.

"Do you always greet women you don't know with a lip-lock, Mr. Logan?"

A smile crinkled the skin at the corners of his eyes. "As a matter of fact, I don't. That was from Don."

"Huh?"

"He said he owed you one from New Year's Eve two years ago and made me promise to deliver it."

She stared up at him in total incomprehension. Logan hooked a brow and attempted to prompt a nonexistent memory.

"He abandoned you at the Waldorf. Five minutes before midnight. To deliver twins."

"I don't have a clue who or what you're..."

Understanding burst like a water balloon.

"Wait a sec. Are you talking about Sabrina's old boyfriend? Your buddy, who's now an ob-gyn doc?"

It was Logan's turn to look startled. He recovered faster than Devon had, though. His smile widened into a rueful grin.

"I take it you're not Sabrina Russo."

"No, Mr. Logan, I am *not*."

* * * * *

Be sure to look for
THE CEO'S CHRISTMAS PROPOSITION
by Merline Lovelace.
Available in November 2008 wherever books are sold,
including most bookstores, supermarkets,
drugstores and discount stores.